"What yuh want, Mister Jervis?"

"Max, can you call the rest of your family? I s'pose your Pa's still bad off, but I want him to hear this too."

"Pa ain't feelin' very pert, Mister Jervis. I'll call the rest though." Max gave a low whistle. From around the house and side sheds came Millie, Kiah and Manny. They lined up solemn as prairie owls.

Millie spoke. "Mister Jervis, set a spell."

"Thank yuh, Millie." Jervis cleared his throat. "Folks, I've knowed you since yuh come t' town. I know you're pretty well growed up. I got bad news but it must be said. Your brother Loper was shot an' killed on the stage south of Willer Springs this mornin'. He was doin' his duty, guarding Mister Denny's box of high-grade. Mister Levi Esch buried him in Willer Springs an' sent a message t' the sheriff."

No one cried. No one moved for a second. Then they all looked to Max. "Maximillian," Millie said, "yer head o' the Bleckers while Pa's ailin'. You'll hafta go help Mister Denny at the Ajax.

"Mister Jervis, thank yuh kindly fer bringin' us this message," Max added. "Tell Mister Levi we'll come over t' thank him an' see Interloper's grave when we kin. We'll tell Pa when he'll lissen. Did Loper do as he was told by Mister Denny?" Max's question was in dead earnest.

"He died doin' what he said he'd do. The bandit killed him because he wouldn't throw the box of gold out on the road."

Other ACE Books by C. R. Clumpner:

KETCH ROPE

SIX
WHO DIED YOUNG

C.R. CLUMPNER

ace books
A Division of Charter Communications Inc.
A GROSSET & DUNLAP COMPANY
360 Park Avenue South
New York, New York 10010

SIX WHO DIED YOUNG

Copyright © 1978 by C. R. Clumpner

An ACE Original

First ACE Printing: September, 1978

Published simultaneously in Canada

Printed in U.S.A.

CONTENTS

Introduction

CHAPTER   **PAGE**

INTRODUCTION

Laid in Northeastern California near the Nevada Territory line, this story covers a relatively short time in the lives of various people living there in the 1870s. Although place names are fictional, the mountains, rivers and juniper flats are still there. Persons with knowledge of the country will recall similar types of terrain in the area.

Intermingling of crime and violence with good will, peace, and faith was characteristic of the times. There were men like Percy Cameron in the cattle country. There are people still living who remember violence and rustling there. Sheriffs failed to do their true duty, and girls like Millie Blecker had choices and decisions to make, dreaming of and hoping for the help and reassurance they needed. Too often it failed to come.

Six Who Died Young was written for one purpose — entertainment. If it serves to pass time away, enlighten, or give some desk-bound reader a vacation, then writing it has been worthwhile.

1

THE HOLDUP

"PUT THAT BOX over the edge an' don't try no tricks."

The speaker and his rough black gelding mount were not quite in the open, but Bledsoe, the stagecoach driver, and the boy beside him could see them behind sagebrush among the junipers. The rider held a sawed-off shotgun low and cocked for action. Across the road, back in the lava, was another man with a gun. They meant trouble.

"Mister, I cain't do it. I promised Mister Denny I'd look out fer this box an' take keer of it."

"I'll make yuh another promise—I'll blow a hole in yer gizzard the buzzards kin see fer a mile if yuh don't kick that box out in the road. Kick it over, I tell yeh, afore I pull the trigger!"

"You'll just hafta pull her then, Mister. I told Mr. Denny I'd look out fer this box an' I mean to do it."

"Listen, yeh silly son-of-a-bitch, turn loose that box. I ain't foolin'."

The driver spoke up. "Push her over, kid. He means it."

"Mr. Bledsoe, I cain't do it. I promised Mr. Denny—"

A rider armed with a rifle, blue neckerchief across his face, pushed his sorrel out in the open from across the road.

"Fer Christ's sake, Ed, shoot the bastard an' let's git on our way. Do somethin' afore we git in deeper'n we are," he urged. "Don't you try any funny business, Bledsoe."

The shotgun roared, blue smoke rolled. The stage driver yelped, and the boy, still holding the box, jerked up, then slumped down in a limp mass, chest and one shoulder shattered. The box tumbled to earth and the stagecoach team reared to run, but the rider of the sorrel caught them.

The man who had fired held his gun at ready. "Jim, git that box," he rasped. "Bledsoe, git the hell on yer way an' don't look back or I'll give yuh the other barrel."

Bledsoe held up his arm. "Gimme time t' plug this hole, willya? I could bleed t' death afore I get to town."

4

"Well, then, bleed t' death. Teach yeh to carry a crazy kid along on a man's job. Git them jugheads poundin' the road." The masked man waved his gun and backed away.

The driver whooped at the team, releasing the brake and pulling hard on his left rein to turn the stage and head back toward Willow Springs. Iron-edged wheels screeched and sparked on gravel and stone, the horses running as the stagecoach circled, lurched back into the straight-away, and clattered off.

The dead boy began to slide forward, and Bledsoe shifted his feet in an attempt to prevent his falling off. After a quarter of a mile he glanced back and saw a huddle of men and horses in the road. Reaching down his bloody right hand, he pulled the body closer to center.

The team ran smoothly until the stage stopped at the bottom of a little grade in answer to Bledsoe's pull at the reins and his soft, "Whoa-up . . . whoa now." Shoving the brake tight with his foot he wrapped reins around brake handle and got down. He pulled the body onto his shoulder, shifted it onto the floor inside the coach. Looking back fearfully he climbed to the driver's seat and with quick movements unwrapped the reins and released the brakes; then he shouted at the team and popped his whip.

Approaching Willow Springs, they made the final run down grade into the main street. Two saloons, one store, a small livery stable, an eating house, post office and rooming house combined. Houses could be counted on the fingers of both hands and people in Willow Springs, gathered together, would number slightly more than fifty.

Postmaster Levi Esch, also liveryman, town marshal, and pawnbroker for cowboys, miners, and half-breed Indians, stood in the street. He had heard the rapid approach of the stage, and wondered apprehensively why it had returned. Bledsoe pulled in a drift of dust. After the stage driver's brief story, Esch asked questions.

"Rufe, how come this feller was riding shotgun for yeh today instead of some older, more experienced man?"

"Hell, Levi, I jest drive this outfit. When I stopped t' pick up the box at the Ajax Mine, Bill Denny says, 'Rufe, Loper here's agreed to take this box through for me. You let him ride up with you, hear?' I let him ride."

"What do yeh figger was in the box?"

"High-grade; what else? Thing weighed fifty pound or more. Non o' my business what he sends, long as he pays the freight."

"Yuh say the kid never tried to shoot? Jest set there and held onta the box an' told the feller to go ahead an' fire, he wasn't going to turn loose?"

"Sure as hell did. Say, Levi, can yuh fix up my arm with liniment or something? I could stand a drink, too."

Levi turned. "Flossie, c'mon out here!" he hollered. "Bring some rags and turpentine." He turned back the driver's sleeve. "Hell, Bledsoe, you're barely scratched. Bled a little, that's all. Let's get back to what happened. You figger it was Slick George and his gang?"

6

"Levi, I ain't sayin' one word about who it mighta been. Hell, I don't want my ears nicked with no Arkansaw toothpick."

"By grab, Rufe, if we don't do somethin' to get rid of that gang, we might all get it. Now who is this young feller and how'd it happen Denny picked him?"

"Name is Loper Blecker—Lope, they called him—oldest one of Looney Blecker's batch. Works like hell-a-mile, but says strictly nuthin'."

"Looney Blecker! That the army captain lives in Hooper's Bend? I heard he's got a busted head, sits in the sun all day back of that river shack the other side of town."

"That's the cuckoo. Got six kids, or did have. Damndest kids to work, but run like rabbits when a stranger shows up. Holy old Moses, Levi! You pourin' on liquid fire? Hold off! Whew! Man-oh-man, that hurts more'n buckshot did. Give me another drink an' don't never pour more o' that stuff on me."

"It's just plain old horse liniment. Takes the posion out of the lead so 'twon't fester and get proud flesh. Only other way I know's with a hot iron."

Bledsoe glared. "What're yuh gonna do with the body?"

"Bury it, I guess. Weather's too hot for it to keep long. S'pose old Blecker'll squawk if we bury Loper here?"

"Nope. He don't know nothin' anyway, an' his kids're too young t' have brains er money. Don't know who'll pay yuh. Charity case, I reckon."

"I'll put in for some money from old man Denny. Get on your way now, and when you come back day after tomorrow I'll have a report. You better write one up too."

"Okay," Bledsoe sighed. "Bury the kid, bill old man Denny, an' fer gosh sakes don't drink none of that liniment. It'll burn yer guts out." He spat and turned to leave.

"You better reckon on what that murderin' outfit looked like, Rufe. If the sheriff ain't interested in their description, Denny will be. So long."

Levi Esch got two half-drunk riders from the saloon to help his crippled stableman dig a grave. The promise of a little cash for more drinks aroused their latent ambition. No one seemed excited over the robbery nor the fact that a young boy had been killed. To the inhabitants of Willow Springs it was but one more incident in the life they knew.

Esch was a Jew. He neither bragged about it nor apologized for it, but did what he had to do and made a living regardless of what people thought. Postmaster because he was the only person in Willow Springs who wanted the job, he also loaned money, and ran the livery stable and boardinghouse. He'd say a prayer over Lope Blecker's body because his religion wouldn't let him put a man in the grave without doing so.

Six people and one dog heard the Bible verses read: Levi's housekeeper, Flossie, Hap the stableman, two cowboys, and Roscoe Eppling, owner of the Rest Easy Saloon and Cardroom, there as official witness that the boy was buried legal. The dog present thought the men were digging out a squirrel. Levi asked the Lord for mercy on the murdered boy's soul.

As the group straggled back to the shelter of the buildings, the dog sniffed at the mound of earth and trotted along.

"We kin git Harry Green t' ride over t' Hooper's Bend an' let the sheriff know what happened; then he kin ride on up to the Ajax and tell Denny what happened," Eppling proposed. "You got a pony for him, Esch?"

Tom Dyer, the sheriff, would huff and puff, brag and blow; what Denny would do was anyone's guess.

"Yeah," Levi agreed. "Say, Roscoe, them renegades that robbed the coach—if they keep on it may be our scalps they hang up t' dry next. Shootin' that boy was a little too much fer me. Sooner er later somebody's got t' stop 'em."

"If I was you, Esch, I'd keep my lip buttoned. We know each other, but I don't know who you know and you don't know who I talk to. Savvy?"

" 'Course I do . . . maybe you're right. Send old Harry over. You furnish him grub money an' I'll furnish the pony."

"Fair enough, Levi."

The road between Willow Springs and Hooper's Bend ran through sand and sagebrush country, scattered juniper, lava rock canyons, and rolling, flattened hills. Harry Green knew it well. He and his hard-mouthed cayuse headed north at three o'clock that afternoon.

Sheriff Tom Dyer, half asleep in his chair of willow sprouts and rawhide when Green rode in on Esch's pony, only came awake when Harry said, "Sheriff, the stage was held up and robbed jist afore it hit Cow Hollow drop. The guard was plugged an' killed. Levi and Eppling buried him. Sent me t' tell yuh about it."

The sheriff straightened. 'Yer name's Green, ain't it?"

"That's me."

"Hell's bells, git off yer pony an' come inside. Where'd yeh git that cayuse?"

"Belongs t' Levi. Eppling give me eatin' money. I'm s'posed to tell yuh if there's a claim against Denny fer the guard's burial, Levi gits his first. He done the job."

"The hell with Levi! If Denny wants t' pay him, well an' good. I ain't puttin' in any claim. Who was the guard?"

"Lope Blecker. I never see him afore. Levi said Rufe Bledsoe told him Denny hired the kid but, hell, it was his own durn foolishness got him killed."

"What d' yuh mean?"

"Rufe said a masked feller ridin' a black gelding shoved a sawed-off shotgun in his whiskers from the sage on the right side o' the road. Rufe stopped the team. Feller tells the kid t' toss out the box he was holdin'. Kid says no. Feller says he'll shoot. Kid says Mr. Denny told him t' look out fer the box an' he cain't do that. Feller on the gelding touched off one barrel and caught the kid dead center. One buckshot scratched old Rufe's arm.''

"Then what?" The sheriff leaned over his desk.

"Got a drink handy, Sheriff? Twenty miles o' alkali dust dries up my whisper.''

The sheriff handed over a bottle. Green took a few swallows and handed it back to Dyer, who quickly corked it and returned it to his desk drawer.

"Well . . . then Rufe kicked over the box. Five or six of the gang scattered out in the lava and yelled at Rufe to git. Rufe got, holdin' the kid on the rig with his foot till he hit the bottom of the hollow, then dumped him inside the stage and come on in. They had him laid out an' buried in no time. I never saw nothin' but some blood on the porch of Levi's boardinghouse. Hell of a note, I say.''

"All the bunch took was the box from the Ajax?"

"Never bothered the mail sacks an' the other packages.'' Green walked to the door, cleared his throat, and spat into the dusty road, then clomped back and wilted into the chair set before the sleepy-eyed sheriff's desk.

"Anybody in Willow Springs take a guess who it was done the job? Levi or Eppling give yuh any ideas?"

"Nope, nobody wanted t' talk. I guess you know why.''

"Yeah . . . darn well. You say you got a message for Denny at the Ajax? Let's see it.''

"Well, I guess it'll be all right, seein' how you're the sheriff an' the law. Levi didn't say nothin' about you readin' it, though.''

"Well, how in hell does he figger I kin find out who held up the goddam stage unless I git all the facts? Trouble with these pot-peddlers, they're allus tryin' t' hide somethin'. C'mon, let's see it.''

The message was written on cheap lined paper torn from a tablet.

Willow Springs, June 15, 1 p.m.

Mr. Denny:

I write to inform you that your faithful guard was shot and killed in a hold-up near Cow Hollow this day. The stage was stopped by outlaws who demanded the box you entrusted to one Lope Blecker, a boy about 16 or 17 years of age. Mr. Blecker refused to comply with their demands and the pleadings of the driver, Rufus Bledsoe. One of the hold-up riders shot him with a sawed-off shotgun loaded with buckshot.

Due to the heat, immediate burial was necessary. Mr. Roscoe Eppling was the witness.

Will you notify next of kin? When you come through Willow Springs you can reimburse me for the expense incurred. There are no apparent clues as to who the robbers were, but the sheriff is being notified.

Y'r obedient servant,

Levi A. Esch, Town Marshal, Willow Springs

Hell, the sheriff thought, *that can't hurt nothin'.*
"Take it an' git on yer way to the Ajax," he said
to Green.

2

LEVI ESCH'S DECISION

THE AJAX MINE lay eleven miles east of Willow Springs. At the edge of Juniper Flats the trail to the mine wound up into scraggly timber through pine flats and benches to the top of the breaks—granite outcroppings, huge boulders and ledges. Trickling springs dropped from canyons into small lakes and swampy pockets. Mineral country.

Bill Denny, coming from the placer region of the Mother Lode, had hit Willow Springs at that cross-trail stop. He went north, prospecting along rough rims that eventually joined the Sierra Nevada, by-passing Hooper's Bend except when short of powder and salt. No longer young, he could live on meat and willow sprouts as long as there was water to wash it down; it took little to sustain him while he followed up traces of color.

Finally, high above the juniper breaks, he found a small showing of gold in granite. He kept prospecting until he located a stringer rich enough to work, trusting the vein would widen and be rich enough in high-grade ore to pay for tunneling as he went. There was no smelter within 200 miles.

He held out for several years, aging under time and labor. Eventually the mine was profitable enough so he could hire someone to come and work for him now and then, enabling him to follow farther gleaming traces and thin, wire-like strands of gold back to their source deep in the mountain.

Denny hired Loper Blecker after glimpsing him in Hooper's Bend one early spring day. He inquired of Jervis, owner of the Hooper's Bend Mercantile, who the kid was.

"That's one of Looney Blecker's kids," Jervis replied. "Oldest one. Ain't that the dangdest name for a kid? Lope, they call him, but it's really Interloper Blecker. Old man Blecker told me how it come about. Tell you about it sometime, if it's handy."

Denny asked if the kid was a worker and what Jervis thought of him.

"Hell, them's the workingest kids ever whelped. They scatter in the morning and look all day for things to carry home at night. Ever see their hogan? It's made of willer poles, hides, logs, canvas and sod. Started out a kind of teepee, kept building on, patching, chinking, and walling-up till they got something like a prairie-dog town above ground." Jervis took a chew of rough-cut tobacco. "You wanted t' know what I think of Lope? If the kid says he'll do something, jest figger it's done. He and all the rest of that litter'll carry out anything they say they will and, mister, that's usually one hell of a lot."

Bill Denny was curious about the Bleckers. When he walked out to where they lived, he was flabbergasted. Jervis' description of a prairie-dog-town kind of place fit. Willows and poles stuck in the ground, bent over and covered with canvas and hides, and from this central room others built on. The east side had a room open to the front like a porch. In the shade there, leaning back in a hand-fashioned chair with deerskins laid over it, Denny saw a man dressed in a worn gray uniform, black whiskers covering his face and throat, feet bare, a few big flies crawling over toes which occasionally wiggled in protest.

Denny was startled by a child's voice. "What yuh want, mister?"

A girl peered from one of the built-on structures, bright hair hanging around her face. Denny was struck by her resemblance to a red fox cub he'd once seen peering at him from a cleft in some rocks, ready to hide in its burrow at any sudden move. In a low voice he asked, "Does Loper Blecker live here?"

"What yuh want Loper fer?"

"My name's Bill Denny. I've got a mine up in the hills. Mr. Jervis said Loper might do some work for me. I pay in gold."

"Money or dust, mister?"

"Either one."

"How much?"

"Two dollars a day at the mine, and his grub."

"When kin he start?"

"Today. I'll pay him half a day's wages."

"Time's money, Paw says. What'll Lope be doin'?"

"Don't you think I better talk to Loper or your father?"

"Nope. Paw ain't feelin' very pert and Lope's down the river, fishin'. I kin say."

"Well, if that's the case, do you mind if we sit down?"

"You go round t'other side an' my sister'll be there."

Denny circled left, amazed at the connected huddle of buildings and shed-like hovels. As he walked around the complex he felt someone watched his progress, perhaps over the muzzle of a gun. On the north side was another open-fronted, willow-thatched shed, another bent willow chair covered with dried deerhides, and a rough bench. From the lower door came another girl, with even brighter red hair.

"Howdy, mister . . . what did yuh say your name was?"

"Bill Denny. What can I call you?"

"You kin call me Millie. That ain't all my name,

though. Millennium, my ma called me. This here's my sister Lou.''

"Millie, you've got quite a home here.''

"You makin' fun of it, mister?''

"Why no, Millie, I think it's unusual. Cool in summer, I'll bet, and warm in winter.''

"Yup. Well, set down, mister. If Lope goes t' work fer yuh, when kin he git paid? I've got t' know—see t' the cookin'.''

"Every week, if he wants it that way.''

"How often will he come in town?''

"Once or twice a month, I reckon. Often enough to bring in a little high-grade for me and get supplies. It's eleven miles out to the mine. I hate to lose any work-time.''

The girl sat on the bench and studied the gray-haired miner. Satisfied, she said, "All right, Mister Denny. When Lope comes he kin go with you.''

"Thank you, Millie. When'll he be back?''

"In half an hour. Wait here.''

She rose, slipped through a doorway hung with a dried cowhide that still had hair on it and disappeared.

Denny tried to figure what went on in this place. There must be other children around. Evidently the old man was still asleep.

Millie was back. She seated herself on the bench. Apparently she made the decisions.

"How many do you have to cook for, Millie?'' Denny asked.

"Seven, countin' Paw. Takes a heap to keep us goin'. Lope an' Max eat like horses when they work, an' perty heavy when they don't. How many up t' yer mine, Mister Denny?''

"There'll be just Loper and me for now. Don't know if I'll hire anyone else.''

"If you need him, Max kin help. He's not so big, but he's strong, and he kin gopher dirt like nobody's business.''

"I'll keep that in mind, Millie. Is that your brother Lope coming?''

"Yup, that's Lope. Jest let me do the talkin'.''

Up from the willows along the river came a fellow not quite a man, but already stooped with a man's burdens. Below the edges of his old black sombrero his hair straggled, long and dark. He wore Levis, checkered shirt, and runover boots with toes scuffed through. Denny had the impression as he approached that the boy was suspicious, reluctant to meet anyone, especially a stranger.

Close to him now, under the roof of the built-on shelter, Denny could see Lope Blecker's light gray eyes, dark lashes and heavy brows. His face, tanned except for a few freckles, had a straight nose and slightly receding jaw. Work-roughened hands hung well out of his sleeves. Denny judged the boy weighed about 140 pounds or so. After a month of good chuck, he'd put on another 20.

"Loper, this here's Mister Denny, come lookin' fer yuh to work fer him,'' Millie said. "He's got a mine up in the hills. He'll pay yuh every week, gold or gold dust, two dollars a day and grub. I told him you'd take the job.''

"That's right, Mister Denny?''

"That's right. Should I call you Loper or Mr. Blecker?''

"Lope's all right. When do I start an' how long will it last?"

"Today, if you can come. There's still time to earn a dollar. I can use you all summer, maybe a lot longer. Up there, I'm like a badger huntin' mice. Kinda like to work all the time."

"Don't mind that. You live in a cabin?"

"Yeah. You got a gun?"

"Gun? What fer?"

"Well, Lope, seems like where there's gold there's always trouble. If we get held up we want something besides talk to answer with."

"Millie, git my things laid out. Reckon I better take a coat. Mister Denny, I'll hafta come back down here next week t' buy grub an' see how Paw an' the kids are. That all right?"

"Loper, we won't have no quarrels about that. I can advance you a week's wages."

"Advance?"

"I give you a week's pay, and you work it out."

"No sir, I couldn't do that. Paw wouldn't like it. I'll do the work first an' do it like you want it."

"Well, that's fine, Loper. I know how you feel."

"Lope, here's yer things. What gun yuh goin' t' take?" Millie came from behind the swinging cowhide with a small rolled-up bundle of clothes.

The boy glanced at her, went inside, and reappeared strapping on a Navy Model Colt.

"Now, Millie, you kin run the place. Take care o' Paw, an' see he don't set out too late. Make sure the mules don't git in the garden. See to it the little fellers git more wood piled up. I'll be back soon as I kin."

There were no farewells. Lope Blecker turned and followed Denny back to town, shouldered his share of supplies, and went along to the hill mine.

Now Loper was dead and buried. When Harry Green got to the mine shack that evening, varied thrushes called under the trees, and shadows covered distant valleys. He found Denny washing up, ready to eat. In the cool, peaceful quiet, the gray-haired, whiskered miner let the breeze dry his damp body.

"What can I do for you, mister? You're welcome to eat and set a spell," he called.

"You Bill Denny an' this the Ajax Mine?"

"That's right."

"Well, I'm Harry Green from Willer Springs. Levi Esch sent me over."

"Something wrong, Green?"

"Mr. Esch sent yuh a message." Green pulled out the paper.

Denny went into his cabin, reappeared with steel-rimmed glasses hung on his nose, and turned his back to the west to get the last light. Slowly he read the note. Green squatted, watching him.

"Mr. Green, is this true?"

"Yeah. Lope was shot with a sawed-off loaded with buckshot. Levi buried him today."

"You've seen the sheriff?"

"I stopped and told him what happened. He asked t' see that there note and I showed it to him."

"Esch say the sheriff was supposed to read it?"

"Nope, but he wanted to. He's the law, so I

guess he had a right to see it, didn't he?"

"Could be. Did anybody tell the Bleckers about what happened to Loper?"

"Nope. Maybe the sheriff will. His job, ain't it?"

"Could be. Well, let's eat. You can stay here tonight. In the morning we'll go back together. I thank you for bringing me the note, Mr. Green."

"Old Levi figgered yuh oughta know about it. That kid was plumb loco t' hang onto the box, wasn't he?"

"It's all in the way you look at it. I guess he figured he was working for me and protecting something I trusted him with. Hell of a note when somebody plugs a boy doin' a man's job! Murders him, I should say. Anybody guess who it was?"

"Nobody, not even me . . . yuh can't trust nobody in Willer Springs—it's even worse in Hooper's Bend. Even the sheriff ain't guessin'."

Denny dished up grub on two tin plates. "Yeah, I can understand that, all right," he grunted.

"How come yuh hired a kid t' ride with the box, Mister Denny?"

"Because I could trust him, that's why. Can you name any other feller would set there and tell a man with a sawed-off shotgun what Lope did? I can't."

"Well, he's deader'n hell now. No use bein' honest if that's what it gets yuh. I'd rather be alive than a corpse."

"Green, you hit the nail on the head. So would most fellers in this country. Every time a good man's killed, two bad ones seem to sprout from the willows. The country's full of bandits, outlaws, brand-burners and horse thieves. Ever think what'll happen when they get the honest men killed off? Well, I have. They'll own the country and enslave the rest of us. Fact is, they're doin' it now.''

Green chewed, took a swallow of coffee. "How do yuh mean?"

"Hell, I slaved and Loper slaved for that gold. They took it. We slaved jest for them, the bastards. No more, I say. They got the last high-grade of mine they're goin' to." He paused, breathed. "Reckon I said too much. To hell with 'em, the sheriff too. Let's eat and hit the soogans. Tomorrow we'll head for Hooper's Bend."

3

JERVIS GOES TO THE BLECKERS'

AFTER HARRY GREEN departed, the sheriff swore
in a few men as a posse and galloped toward the
place the stage had been held up, having told Ben
Jervis, who ran Hooper's Bend Mercantile, to let
the Bleckers know Lope had been killed and
buried in Willow Springs.

Jervis took off the apron that protected his suit,
put a derby hat on his balding head, left his wife to
watch the store, and headed toward the Bleckers'
place. In the hot sun, sand slipped underfoot, he

sweated, wondering what he would say to the family. Cap'n Blecker was ailing, unable to listen let alone talk to anyone.

Knowing the strange wild flock of Blecker children better than most people in Hooper's Bend, Jervis realized anything he said might heighten their suspicion. Maybe they would feel he was an enemy along with everyone else.

He thought back to when they had first came to town. Two years before, late in the fall after several killing frosts, two wagons drawn by big, rawboned, long-eared mules, and driven by long-haired boys who said they were from "back south," rolled into Hooper's Bend. They passed slowly through town and stopped at the river near a heavy patch of willows. There the wagons' occupants began to build a home.

It was two weeks before townspeople knew how many humans made up the Blecker household. After that, it became generally known that old "Cap'n" Blecker wasn't often rational and able to talk, and the spells that took him grew more frequent and lasted longer. Doc Brown said he'd been injured in the war and his brain was softening. He was the father, but there was no mother. Somebody heard one of the kids say she got bit up high by a rattler while squatting in the weeds one night. The kids raised themselves until Cap'n Blecker came home from the war and then they had him to take care of.

Loper and Max, the two oldest boys, had heard of the California gold country and how land could be had for the taking. From then on it was a family affair. They tried everything to get money and a way to haul what little they had to the promised land. Finally, a settler wanted their acreage. Their paw, who happened to be rational that day, signed over his land in exchange for the settler's extra wagon and team of mules. With their own team and what they had, the Bleckers started northwest.

Loper drove one team and the lead wagon, Max drove the other. With Loper were his father and the boy named Emancipation, Manny for short; in the second wagon, Max driving, with Hexikiah to spell him, were the two girls, Millié and Lou. The outfit drove well over two thousand miles before they reached Hooper's Bend, an accomplishment as hard to believe as the children's unusual names. Lou was really Louisiana, Millie's given name, Millennium; Maximillian was the next, then Interloper. But the children were proud of their names, firmly believing in their mother's choice.

All this went through Ben Jervis's mind as he walked the hot dusty road. Lou saw him coming and stayed near the west door until he was within speaking distance. Beside her, her brother Max spoke first.

"What yuh want, Mister Jervis?"

"Max, can you call the rest of your family? I s'pose your Pa's still bad off, but I want him to hear this too."

"Paw ain't feelin' very pert, Mister Jervis. I'll call the rest though." Max gave a low whistle. From around the house and side sheds came Millie, Kiah and Manny. They lined up solemn as prairie owls.

Millie spoke. "Mister Jervis, set a spell."

"Thank yuh, Millie." Jervis cleared his throat. "Folks, I've knowed you since yuh come t' town. I know you're pretty well growed up. I got bad news but it must be said. Your brother Loper was shot an' killed on the stage south of Willer Springs this mornin'. He was doin' his duty, guarding Mister Denny's box of high-grade. Mister Levi Esch buried him in Willer Springs an' sent a message t' the sheriff."

No one cried. No one moved for a second. Then they all looked to Max. "Maximillian," Millie said, "yer now head o' the Bleckers while Paw's ailin'. You'll hafta go help Mister Denny at the Ajax."

"Mister Jervis, thank yuh kindly fer bringin' us this message," Max added. "Tell Mister Levi we'll come over t' thank him an' see Interloper's grave when we kin. We'll tell Paw when he'll lissen. Did Loper do as he was told by Mister Denny?" Max's question was in dead earnest.

"He died doin' what he said he'd do. The bandit killed him because he wouldn't throw the box of gold out on the road."

"Mister Jervis, I'll come by the store at sun-up an' go up t' the mine. I wish you'd send a note t' Mister Levi an' tell him we'll pay him."

"I'll do that, Max. Are you sure yuh want to work for Mister Denny?"

"Loper did. I kin take his place. Mister Denny needs someone. I'm the oldest now. Millie kin take keer of the place an' look after Paw."

"That's right, Mister Jervis. Max, yuh better git

things ready t'night an' leave early."

Jervis walked back to his store in sand and heat. What would happen to the Bleckers now? How much longer would Cap'n Blecker live on, half-animated flesh that ate and slept, groaned, and moved only with someone else as guide? The burden of sustaining his life was on his children and the responsibility of doing what they'd been taught to do grew greater as time went on.

The sheriff and his five-man posse stopped where the hold-up had taken place. In the dusty road the heat was stifling. Wheelmarks and tracks showed where horses and stagecoach had stood, the team plunging in their turnaround. They found where the bandits had concealed themselves, smoked and loafed until the stage appeared. An empty whiskey bottle shimmered in the sun.

"Five of 'em here. Busted the box that the kid got plugged fer not kickin' over. Crazy galoot," Sheriff Dyer grumbled as he walked back and forth looking for more clues.

"Wonder how much that box o' gold was worth. Not enough to git killed fer, I'll bet. Them fellers knew their business though. Joe yuh pick up any ideas?"

"Nope, not enough t' say who 'twas. Be dark in a few hours. If we're gonna trail 'em, we got t' git busy."

"Hell, I kin tell yuh from right here without movin' a step jest what'll happen. They'll ride straight fer the ridge headed northwest. They'll cross Wolf Gap an' be in lava country. We'll make the gap t'night, camp at the seep where grass is good an' by ten o'clock the next day we'll give up an' head back east to the Bend. Damn them fellers fer doin' a job when the weather's hot. Tom, whatcha make of this hold-up, anyway?''

''Plain ol' case o' Denny tryin' t' ship a box of gold out and not giving it any protection. What else could it be?''

''Hell, how'd these fellers know it was goin' out? You figger somebody tipped 'em off?''

''Yeah. Who it was we have t' find out.''

Milling around a few minutes longer and finding no more evidence, they headed northwest across sagebrush country. The bandits' trail was easy to follow. Just as the sheriff predicted, the posse camped that night at a little spring seeping from under a lava flow, trickling down through sedge and willows. At daylight they once more took the trail.

The posse wandered out to search in the lava rock, looked for signs, found less and less of them, had a few half-hearted arguments and squabbles, then headed back for the Hooper's Bend Bar, agreeing they could do nothing more to identify or capture the robbers.

On their ride to Hooper's Bend, Denny in the lead and Harry Green following on Levi's horse, they spotted a traveler heading their way at six-thirty in the morning. Denny was surprised to see Max Blecker. ''Good morning, boy,'' he said, ''looking' for me?''

"Yeah, Mister Denny. I come t' go to work."

"You must have heard about Loper. I'm sorry, boy. Never figgered that would happen."

The boy looked at the aging man. "Neither did we, Mister Denny. Somebody's got t' take Loper's place. Reckon it's me—I'm the oldest."

"Well, Max, I'm headed to the Bend to see Sheriff Dyer and then I was goin' to see you folks. You want to work for me in Loper's place, do you?"

"Yup. Millie said she'd take keer of things at home."

"Okay, you go on up to the mine. I left the cabin unlocked. Fix yourself some grub, rustle wood. You could go down the ridge toward dark and kill a piece o' meat. But mind, don't shoot anything closer than half a mile. The close ones are for in case I need one quick. Wait for me."

The men rode on, Green to Willow Springs, while Denny stopped off at Hooper's Bend to see the sheriff. Not finding Dyer back from the manhunt, he went next door to the Jervis Mercantile Company.

"Ben, what do you know about Loper's killing?"

"Only what I heard from Green and Dyer. Should hear some more when the sheriff comes back from chasing shadows and campin' out."

"Have you seen the Bleckers? I met Max this morning up the trail. Said Millie told him to take Loper's place, and I thought, *What in hell*? Guess he figures he's a grown man now his brother's gone."

"He is, too. Them Bleckers ain't whimperin', pulin' kids, even Manny. Never batted an eye ner dropped a tear when I told 'em about Loper. Dangdest thing I ever seen. Give me the willies."

"Yeah, reckon it would. I took quite a likin' to Loper up there at the mine. Never said more'n a few words at a time but what he said made sense. I never did git under his skin, though. How they fixed for money?"

"You know as much about that as I do, Denny. Not very well, I reckon. Don't see how they could have anything laid by."

"Well, I'll go on out there. There's money due 'em—Loper's wages."

Denny saw Manny, playing lookout, disappear around the shanty. Millie appeared and greeted him.

"Mister Denny, we're sure sorry Lope got killed an' lost yer box o' gold. I sent Max up to work in his place."

"Yes, Millie, I saw him. I'm sorry Lope got killed, too. How will you get along without your brother?"

Millie looked up at him. "We don't worry, Mister Denny. We kin git along. If Paw was better, it'd help. But if Max kin work, everything'll be fine."

"I brought you Loper's pay, Millie. It ain't so much, but it'll help." He handed her a battered leather pouch. "If Max can stay up there and one of you could come up for his pay, he could get in more time. Maybe that's asking too much, though."

"Oh no, it ain't, Mister Denny! I kin come—maybe Lou. We'll bring yer mail—supplies, too."

"You might try it. Suppose I leave a note with Mister Jervis at the store with something for you to bring. He'll tell you when to come. Better figure on staying the night. Then I'll cook a meal."

"No, if I er Lou come up, we kin cook. That way we kin pay fer our grub." Millie was definite, not to be indebted to anybody for anything.

"Well . . . is there anything I can do for you or the cap'n?"

"Nope. If Max don't do what you want him to, jest let me know, I'll see that he does."

"Oh, Max and I'll get along all right. I better go now—I want to see the sheriff before I head back to the mine. Keep your eyes and ears open, Miss Millie, for anything about who the bandits might be. Let me know. Don't tell anybody else."

"I won't, Mister Denny. I don't know who done it, but we'll find out."

"Listen, girl—be careful. Be sure nobody knows what you're up to. Might get you or me shot. Somebody might be real mean, especially if they figure you want to know."

Her level gaze held his. "Good-bye, Mister Denny. Tell Max we'll make it fine."

"Good-bye, Millie, Mind now, keep it quite." With these words Denny headed back to the store, like Jervis, half-depressed, half-worried about Looney Blecker's kids. But what could he do? Just sit and wait and watch.

Denny gone, the kids clustered around their sister. "What'd he want, Millie? What'd he mean—

be careful? How much money did he give yuh?''

"Wait till I count it, I'll tell yuh what he said an' what I'm going' t' do, but not now. Git to yer jobs."

Millie sat down to count the money and figure what little she could buy at the store. After that, she began to think how she could help Mr. Denny find the outlaws.

4

THE COWBOY AND THE MINER

AMOS BLECKER AWOKE feeling refreshed and clear-headed. He looked off across the river to sun-ripened wild oats and cheat grass. Trees were in full leaf, and the sun's heat, the shimmering haze over sage and juniper, told him summer lay on the land.

Cap'n Blecker knew he was in no condition to do more than talk with his children about what they could accomplish in the way of making a living. Lying in his shaded split-willow chair he again contemplated ending his life, but cast aside the idea. Maybe these spells would end someday, maybe he could find a doctor who could help him end these long, troubled sleeps.

He got up cautiously. No pain in his head, no dizziness—he felt hungry and weak in the legs. He stepped toward the door as Millie came out.

"Why, Paw! Yer up. Yuh feel all right?"

"Feel fine, girl, jest fine. What's there to eat?"

"Cornbread . . . we got some beef stew, an' Kiah kin ketch a trout er two. I'll make some coffee."

"Sounds good, Millie. How long I been sick?"

"I hate t' tell yuh, Paw. A long time. More'n two weeks. But yuh wasn't bad this time. You wasn't no trouble. Don't worry about it, Paw." Millie went to her father and put her arms about him, close to tears.

"Well, that's fine," he reassured her. "Let's go inside. While I eat that stew an' drink some good coffee, you can tell me all that's been goin' on. How's everybody?"

"Jest fine. Ever'body's down by the river 'cept Max an' Loper. You set while I git the coffee goin'."

Millie knew that if her father ate his meal without worry he would remain rational longer. Out of a hole in the wall called a window she saw Lou and motioned for her to leave. Her younger sister didn't question the order but turned, bare feet making no sound in the hot sand.

As he ate and drank, Blecker and his daughter talked about the mules, the garden, how things in town were going, about everything but what had happened to Loper. But when her father had wiped the last drops of coffee from mustache and whiskers, Millie sat down close to him.

"Paw, I want yuh t' lissen t' me. Loper went t' work fer Mister Denny who owns Ajax Mine up on Ragged Ridge. Mister Denny sent him on the stage with a box o' high-grade ore to the assay office. On the road below Willer Springs robbers held 'em up. Loper wouldn't give up the box, so they shot him. Rufe, the stage driver, took him to Willer Springs and Mister Esch buried him. Nobody knows who 'twas robbed the stage. Mister Jervis, he come down and talked t' me, Mister Denny too, and Max went t' take the job Loper had. The sheriff's lookin' fer the hold-up men."

Stunned, Cap'n Blecker sat silent. How helpless he'd become, he thought—his oldest son had been killed, and here he was hearing it for the first time. How could these children live, let alone feed and care for their helpless father? Alert now, and grim, he faced the task ahead.

"Millie, when did it all happen?"

"Four days back, Paw. I told Mister Jervis and Mister Denny t' thank Mister Esch fer taking keer o' Loper an' that when we come through Willer Springs we'd pay fer it. You remember Mister Jervis, don't yuh, Paw?"

"Yes, I remember Ben well."

"Kin I trust him, Paw?"

"Prob'ly as fur as anyone."

"Got t' ask somebody about things, Paw. Mister Denny cain't be here very often."

"Millie, do you remember how long I was all right last time I really talked with you an' Loper?"

"Yes . . . 'bout all one day. Then yuh fell down an' went t' sleep. You jest come awake awhile ago, all right again."

"Lissen, honey, I used t' hope I'd git well. Now I don't know. Sometimes I feel I'll keep on gettin' worse. Has a doctor come to see me?"

"No, Paw. One stopped at the store, but Mister Jervis didn't ask him t' come down, said somebody told him it was no use. The doc jest got back on the stage an' left.

"He was prob'ly right, but let's not worry about that. I'm thinkin' how you children can get along. You got any plans made?"

"Yes, I have. Max is workin' fer Mister Denny, gits two dollars in gold ever' day. We kin all live on less'n two bits a day. I been savin' up so we kin move on er buy land here. Mister Jervis said people in town might make us move from here. Kiah kin git a job cleanin' spittoons fer the Travelers' Rest, an' sweepin' out Mister Jervis's store. Lou cleans house in town now an' then, but it's perty hard work. Right now the three of 'em are cuttin' willers fer chairs an' draggin' wood when they ain't in the garden workin'."

"Good, Millie . . . did you get a milk cow? I recollect we talked of that once."

"No. Loper gittin' killed kinda stopped that. I kin try again, though, with the money I got."

"We still have the two mule teams, don't we? Did you an' the boys consider tradin' one team an' a wagon for a cow?"

"Yeah, but if we had t' move on, we'd need both teams."

"You better figger on livin' here, Millie. Trade or sell one team an' wagon, and get a milk cow, a young one bred so she'll calve in early spring. She'll eat less'n the mules and keep yuh in milk an' butter. Maybe Mister Jervis would look fer a piece of land we could homestead. He'd help you make out the papers. Next time I'm right in the head, I kin sign 'em. Do it soon, Millie. We don't have too much time."

"All right, Paw, we'll do it. Mister Jervis might have some idees fer us. Max's gone, but Kiah an' Manny kin help me. Should I ask the sheriff, too? He might help us find a homestead."

"Millie, I don't trust him, for some reason. Don't let the sheriff know much about our business. Is Denny honest?"

"I think so, Paw. Loper trusted him. He come right down t' see us when he heard what happened, said he wanted us t' keep ears an' eyes open fer the fellers shot Lope an' stole his gold, an' be careful who we talked to."

"How old is Denny?"

"Oh, he's old. Hair an' whiskers almost white. Must be over sixty."

"Well, honey, use judgment. You have to trust somebody, sometime. Has the Bend got a church or preacher yet?"

"No, but Mister Jervis told me a preacher come through headed fer the mines an' said he'd write the Methodists an' tell 'em the town needed a church. Methodists all right, Paw?"

"It don't matter too much which church, honey, long as the preacher's all right, good an' kind an' tolerant. Find that out afore yuh make up yer minds."

"If he comes, Paw, we'll all go t' church."

"Millie, be sure an' take keer of the little box with the family Bible and records. Now git the rest of the children. I want t' talk to 'em."

" 'Course, but I jest wanta tell yuh they still feel kinda bad about Loper. Paw, do you think God wanted it to happen?"

"Yes, Millie, I suppose in His plan there was somethin' He needed Loper fer, so He just come an' got him. What He does is far beyond us mortals."

At the door, Millie whistled the low call of the valley quail: "Chi-ca-go, chi-ca-go." From the willows came an answer.

Amos Blecker remained alert and upright all afternoon. He talked with his children about the past, asked questions concerning their work and their plans for the future. They ate their evening meal together. The sun was down, twilight cool on the river, when the children saw their father double over and clutch his head. Kiah and Millie helped him to his bed. Paw was ailing once more.

Levi Esch received a letter from Denny in answer to his note on the day Loper was shot. Denny thanked him for taking care of the boy's burial and assured Esch that when he came through Willow Springs he would pay him what he was out in time and money, adding that he would like to talk with Esch then.

The sheriff and his posse came around after their foray into the lava country for clues. Nobody in Willow Springs could help. Rufe Bledsoe's description told of fellows with faces well covered; he had recognized nobody behind the muzzles of sawed-off shotguns and .45s.

Esch knew Rufe thought more of staying alive than of being a dead hero, and would not say much about what he had seen. He would give no opinion unless the right person and the right time came so he could feel safe; then if Rufe knew that person was tough and rough enough to hunt down the stage-robbing outlaws he would recall little things that might help.

Rufe Bledsoe was a rough character. He had no reason to be otherwise. He cussed, chewed, and spat; he raised hell after payday. He slept with squaws, dancehall girls, and every loose woman he could persuade. Yet he was good with horses, could get more miles out of the stage team than anyone else, and no one had ever called him a liar.

It was Denny who wondered about Rufe's nerve for battle. Esch talked to him. "Mister Denny," he declared, "Rufe's alive. Someday you or some other feller'll want to know jest what happened out there in Cow Hollow. Rufe might turn the trick, don't forget that."

"You figger Bledsoe wasn't buffaloed, then?"

"Sure, Rufe was buffaloed," Jervis put in, "but he can still look and listen, and he might even talk to the right feller someday. It'll have to be the right feller, though, because Rufe likes to live too well. He ain't sure of Heaven."

"Well, I'll head back to my hole in the hills," Denny said. "Next time I have a poke full of high-grade to take out, I'll arrange things different. Now about the Blecker kids, a week from Sunday you have a couple of 'em fetch me and Max some stuff they can pack on those long-eared mules of theirs."

"Yeah, I'll bet they could hang a coupla gunnysacks on one and ride the other," Jervis agreed.

"I'll tell Millie about it," Esch added.

They figured out what the kids would bring, and then Denny headed back to the Ajax Mine. "So long," he said. He had a sack of groceries and his back was bowed, but his head was up, his eyes bright. He was determined to figure out a way to haul his high-grade past the outlaws. And he wanted to help the Bleckers.

Just before Denny reached the trail that went up from the sage flats, he saw a cloud of dust ahead, and heard the muffled bawling of a herd of moving cattle. He looked for the outrider leading the drive, and saw a tall rider on a big buckskin bronc just ahead.

"Mister," the cowboy called, "I got trouble comin' behind me. You better stick with me until they get by—either that or shinny up a juniper."

"Got some snuffys comin'?"

"Snuffys is right. Some of these shinny-brush critters ain't never seen a man with two legs. They act up enough when they see a man on a horse, but my God, mister, a man walkin'—that'd make 'em blow snot and run yuh down in no time. They got eyes like spyglasses and tempers like red Irishers."

"By grab, you're right." They moved closer together, a big twisted juniper between them and the herd. "Where yuh from?"

"Over in the flats near the desert. Come up from Walker River country. The boss's got a ranch about fifty miles ahead, and he's gonna use these for stockers, get a calf crop or two, then start drivin' 'em up to Idaho. Climb up, mister, and I'll hand yup your sack. Where you headed?"

"I got a gopher hole up in the hills, a little showin' of gold. The Ajax, I call it. I'm Bill Denny."

"Hell yuh have! Makin' any money?"

"No, but I keep a-diggin'. Who're you workin' for?"

"Brand is the BMT—Blake, Muffer and Tooney, a fair-sized outfit, 'bout five thousand head. My name's Cameron. Say, any women in this town might help a few of us boys spend a happy night?"

"Yeah. They'll fix you in the Bend, all right. But don't show any loose money or talk too much. The sheriff's rough on outsiders. If you need anything or want help, see Ben Jervis at the Mercantile. I guess he'd be honest an' fair."

"Thanks, Dad. Here they come! Don't move or they'll root out the tree tryin' to get at yuh."

5

CAMERON MEETS THE BLECKERS

LEAVING THE OLD MAN perched in the tree, the cowpuncher called Cameron rode on ahead of the cattle. The wild-eyed, snuffing cows streamed along, heads down, pushed forward by riders with double ropes and long, braided cowhide bullwhips. The herd, made up of young cows and heifers as stockers for a grass ranch, were all colors, small and fleet as blacktail bucks, sharp-horned, wet-nosed, slab-sided, and nervous as hogs at butchering time.

Cameron saw the smoke of Hooper's Bend and swung west to avoid the town. His crude map told him to cross the river east of the bluffs and make camp where junipers began along the lava rocks, two or three miles from the bright lights and saloons. Just right to ride in for an evening's frolic.

Getting on into the afternoon, the cattle were beginning to slow down, the bunch-quitters pretty well in line. As the herd drifted along in good shape, Cameron saw the river ahead, then stopped and stared.

Right in the trail before him was the doggonedest set of hogans he'd ever seen in all his cowboy days. His buckskin mount braced his legs and bowed his neck, nostrils fluttering, eyes rolling, ears flipping back and forth. From the doorway of one of the built-on rooms came a girl, a shotgun in her hands. What attracted the attention of the buckskin's rider was not the fact she carried a gun, nor her outlandish home. He marveled at the girl's beautiful, bright-red hair that glowed in the sun, loose and flowing to below her shoulders. Cameron sat open-mouthed, stupefied at the sight of her.

"Mister, are those yer cows behind yuh?"

Still Cameron stared. He saw the ragged cotton dress that reached barely to her knees, her legs, scratched and burned brown by the sun, her feet, bare in the sand, her slender body and the outline of small out-thrust breasts. The face . . . almost oval, clean line of chin and jaws, gray-green eyes beneath thin-lined brows, maybe freckles. But that hair! It rippled and quivered with a living glow.

"Well, iffen those are yer cows, yuh got t' see they don't git in our garden." Cameron heard the gun's hammers click as the girl's right hand moved to cock them.

"Sorry, ma'am. I was so durned surprised I couldn't answer. Yeah, the cows belong to my outfit. Nobody told me you lived here. Can I get around your place and still ford the river?"

"Swing wide. See that cottonwood tree with the busted top, the one with the dead limb pointin' north? Yuh kin cross there perty easy. Where yuh gonna bed the critters down?"

Cameron would have to hurry to swing the herd, but this girl fascinated him. Woman hungry, he wanted to sit and look at her and her shining hair.

"Somewhere over across there, I reckon. Any ideas?"

"Clost t' that steeple o' lava rock down the river there's good feed and a nice place t' camp. Snakes in the rocks, though. Mister, yuh better head those critters away from here afore they raise hell with our garden. What's yer outfit?"

"The BMT—Blake, Muffer and Tooney. I'm Cameron, the boss of this little bunch. Well, thanks, ma'am. Who can I say you are?"

"Millie Blecker. Cap'n Amos Blecker's my father."

"Goodbye, Millie. See yuh sometime when I don't have to hurry." Cameron put spur to the buckskin and the pony turned, scattering dust and sand.

Millie stood holding the gun, strangely disturbed.

Men in town had looked at her lately in a peculiar way, and sometimes she resented it. This rider's look of open-mouthed amazement had disturbed but not displeased her. What was different about him? A stranger, tall, bearded, much like any rider with the cattle outfits; but there was something about him that made a difference.

The sun was low. Lou and Manny came out to watch the herd stream by in the dust. Across the river they would feed and drift to bed-grounds for the night.

"Millie, s'pose we could get a cow from that outfit?"

"No, Lou, I don't reckon so. Those range cows're wild as pigs in the bottoms at home, and they don't milk good. Paw said to git a heifer, er a cow bred to calve early so we'd have milk."

Percy Cameron herded the cattle to the river. They drank, then waded across to scatter and feed on the other side while he rode quickly up to where the wagon could stop and make camp for the night, impatient to be done. The more he thought about the red-haired girl, the more anxious he was to stop and see her again.

Thirty years old, Cameron had been working for the BMT three years. He had remained single, having almost given up finding a woman he wanted to marry. Known to be a heller with the girls, and meaner than a snake-bit dog when tricked, he was flush with his money when drunk but a man to tie to in trouble. He had headed west from Illinois through Texas to California; then dropped back to the south country where he met BMT bosses buying cattle. He had no more idea of his future than any other boy in the outfit. Follow the cattle and the grass, maybe someday find a little valley, start with a clean hide and a hot iron, and build up a little spread on the side. A woman? In this country, women were scarcer than honest sheriffs. Let the women stay in town with the whiskey. Better to buy butter than to own a milk cow, anyway.

In Hooper's Bend the news that a herd of cattle and their handlers had bedded down across the north fork was circulating. The town could expect a little trade before morning.

Flora Miller heard about the BMT cowboys. Flora's place over the Bar Nothing Saloon and Cardrooms, had stairways outside and inside for her customers. The place had rooms for cooking and eating, four small cubbyholes where the girls entertained customers, one parlor for introductions and waiting, and a large, mirrored room for special parties.

Flora, a gold-digging, conniving harridan, had someone with influence and money behind her. Buckeroos and traveling prospectors found to their sorrow that if cheated or robbed in her house they would be better off to get out of town and forget it. Flora Miller had many enemies, didn't try to be honest, and didn't need respect, her motto being, "Let's see the color of yer money, mister."

Heinie, her blond, buxom girl of Germanic extraction, had a happy-go-lucky disposition and was most in demand when the crowd was full of whiskey.

Mexia, small, dark, and from below the border,

was like taking a drink mixed with chili pepper. She could dance, sing, romp, and tease.

Marie, supposed to be French, was more Spanish than Mexia. If a man got lonesome and began to drink and mourn, Marie was the one to sit with him for hours, and Flora made certain the fellow paid enough to make up for lost time.

The color that made Alice a redhead came from a bottle and stained the pink-flowered porcelain washbowl a shade that never rinsed free. Under gaslights, Alice's hair looked beautiful and so did she, but in the hard light of day her hair looked like strands of frayed rope, and she seemed old and beaten.

Flora Miller's place was a place of shadows. Even when all the lights were lit, heavy red drapes over the windows, dark-patterned rugs and shaded lamps made it dim. If a man dropped a two-and-a-half-dollar gold piece on the floor he'd have to search on hands and knees to find it. The cubbyholes called rooms were draped. Noise was soaked up like a sponge and so was any blood that might be spilled.

Cameron rode into Hooper's Bend on his roan roping horse. He wanted to stop at Blecker's but it was almost dark and he had other things to do. At Jervis's store he threw his reins over the pole in front, then walked up on the porch into the still-open store.

Weighing out beans, Ben Jervis heard the clump of hard heels. He saw a tall cowboy coming toward him. One gun, big gray hat, leather batwings, silver conchos, a red neckerchief around his throat.

"What kin I do fer yuh, mister? Grub er clothes?"

"You Mr. Jervis?" The cowpuncher's voice was low.

"Yeah."

"A whiskered old miner named Denny come by our herd, told me if I got into trouble or wanted help to see you. My name's Cameron. I work for the BMT Cattle Company out of Carson City. Thought I'd stop to see you before trouble hit me."

"Well, Denny's a friend of mine. You can find trouble here, Cameron. What yuh lookin' for?"

"Oh, the usual—women, whiskey, and a little hell-raisin'."

"Over the Bar Nothing there's a house with four girls. Flora Miller runs it. Don't take any chances with that old dried-up piece of cowhide. She's mean and slick. She'll get your dough and you'll end up dry and broke with a head yuh could sell for a balloon to the French Army. She's got good girls, though. The saloon has whiskey, wines and beer, and it's a good place to get in a fight. The sheriff's office is right across the road, behind it the jail. It's plumb empty now, waitin' for somebody."

"They should've named this place Hooper's Rat-Trap, not Hooper's Bend. What's it cost to get outa the can if you're throwed in?"

"Real money. High as fifty bucks. I ain't the sheriff. Yuh just want to step soft and quiet-like."

"And that house over the saloon?"

"A buck a throw for the girls. Whiskey, two-bits, and cards, not much more. All night deal."

"Cheaper for half-a-dozen boys to buy the house?"

"Might be, Cameron."

The range man stood thinking about the evening ahead, the night of pleasure long denied. Jervis sized him up, wondering why Denny had sent him here.

"Mister Jervis, west of town this afternoon I run into the doggonedest set of hogans I ever saw, down by the river. I expected to see a buncha Digger Indians, but I saw one of the pertiest girls I ever hope to see. Red-haired. You know her?"

"Yeah, I know her."

"I never seen any woman or girls either, with hair like that. Looked like red gold. What about her? What's she doing in that mess of sheds and willow houses? Does she have any kinfolk?"

"Cameron, her name is Millie Blecker. Her paw's almost insane . . . looney. Her oldest brother was killed by hold-up men less'n a week ago. She's tryin' to raise three other kids an' take care of her paw."

Cameron stared. "Jervis, thanks a lot. Good night." He went to the saloon with ideas in his head that did not concern Flora and her girls.

6

THREE BLECKERS AT THE AJAX

CAMERON TOOK HIS herd northwest into the lava and crossed back into flat pine-and-bunchgrass country where there was plenty of feed for the rest of the summer and where BMT had holdings and permanent housing for their men. That autumn the herd would be moved south to winter on lake bottoms and meadows.

There had been no trouble in the Bend. Cameron had seen to that. He let Flora know he and his men would be back later, after setting up at a permanent ranch farther north. Rousty Collins, who owned the Bar Nothing Saloon below Flora, also knew he could expect their trade later. With the idea that the town would have another crack at the waddies, they were allowed to enjoy themselves without having their pockets picked or skulls cracked.

Jervis heard the bunch leave at midnight, popping a few shots, shouting farewells, promising to return. He heard Mexia's squeals as a last kiss was attempted. Would Cameron's crew make a return visit to Hooper's Bend? Somehow he couldn't shake the feeling that Cameron was determined to involve himself in the Bleckers' affairs. Just how, he had no idea.

Kiah and Lou chose Jack and Judy, the gray mules, for their trip to the Ajax. Pads were put on their backs, two gunnysacks tied together slung over their withers. Early Sunday morning, Mr. Jervis helped divide and load store supplies and gave the young Bleckers a map he'd made to guide them to the mine. They set out on their great adventure.

Traveling across sagebrush and juniper country they looked east to upthrusts of lava and granite that marked the north-and-south range. They could see long stretches of pine-covered ridges, the summer range of mule deer that later would drift ahead of winter snow and feed on the flats. There were trout streams high up there, huckleberries, bears, and cougar, a far wilder country than they knew.

It was no trouble to follow the trail. Even when it forked, they knew enough to swing south and keep climbing to the cool air of pine country, where they saw deer and a few grouse at a spring. They let the mules drink and after the brief stop kicked their hard heels into the animal's ribs to push them out on the trail.

From the ridge where he could look down into the valley, Mr. Denny spotted two gray mules coming and went back to his cabin, satisfied. Since Max had joined him, he had developed a paternal interest in all the young Bleckers. Concerning Max, old man Denny was no fool, even though people might have thought he was. In the long run he would come out ahead. The old man had a reason for paying two dollars a day to a kid when a dollar was big wages. With a man around, he might expect to pay with his life once the fellow knew how rich the vein of ore was. All that mattered to Max was to have grub, a place to sleep, and two dollars every day he worked.

The mine was deep. They had to use candles and Max held the steel while the old man swung the sledge. Hour after hour in the cramped tunnel the boy knelt and turned the drill steel in his hands, eyes averted from steel fragments that flew from the shaft and hammer. Denny stopped only to place new holes. Days passed before they finished.

Now Max learned about powder, as he watched Denny load the holes with the black stuff, tamp it tight, a little fuse left out to light. One by one the holes were made into potent charges. The day before the kids were due with the supplies, Denny touched them off.

"Fire in the hole!" he called from the tunnel mouth. "Fire in the hole!"

Max was crouched behind a pine tree, shivering a little. A quick shudder of the ground, a rumble, then another shudder. Denny counted out the shots. "One, two, three, four, five, six . . . seven. That's all, boy. Let's eat and let the smoke clear out."

Early the next morning, candles lighted, they walked into the tunnel, the smell of powder strong and heavy. At the scattered rubble of the blast, Max was anxious to go farther but Denny was examining fragments in the light of his candle, putting them in a small bucket.

"Max, we did a durn good job. S'pose you get the barrow and bring it in. We'll load it and you can wheel it out. I'll pick out what we want to ship."

Denny crawled over the pile of rubble, looking for the vein. Much muck would have to be moved before he could locate it. But they had sure extended the tunnel. If the yield got richer they'd be in pretty good shape.

By the time the Blecker kids arrived, Denny had sorted out enough high-grade to give him an idea of what he had. Lou and Kiah sorted more rocks and Denny resorted them, washing off the muck in a wooden trough by the spring, hefting each piece as he looked for color. By noon he had fifty pounds of material he wanted to send out. Then it was time to eat.

They ate the venison steak, spuds, sourdough bread and coffee in a hurry, interested in getting back to work. Max took the wheelbarrow into the tunnel while the other kids sorted more rocks.

By four in the afternoon, the mules were loaded, the kids ready to return. Denny wrote a note to Jervis and one to Millie, and told Lou and Kiah to say nothing to anyone about the ore on the mules. They were to pile it out of sight in their hogan and come back in two weeks unless they heard different.

After Lou and Kiah left that Sunday morning, Millie hoed in the garden. Manny scooted along on hands and knees, weeding carrots and beets. On this hot day, Millie wanted to get the work done early. Monday she'd have to help old Mrs. Blakely wash, Tuesday it would be ironing, Wednesday she'd be housecleaning for Mrs. Warren, Thursday sewing for Mrs. Jervis, and Friday housecleaning for the Laytons. Saturday was her day to bake and cook at home.

The sun poured down on the sandy garden patch. Manny gave up and went down to the river to swim. Cap'n Blecker lay in his split-willow chair and Millie hoed corn, busy until she heard a horse blow dust from its nostrils.

From over the split rail and woven willow fence, a tall, smooth-shaven cowboy smiled down from his buckskin horse. Suddenly Millie realized how she looked, barefooted, barelegged, patched cotton dress wet with perspiration, hair stringing down her back, face sweaty and grimed. She wished the ground could swallow her.

"Mornin', ma'am. Looks like yuh got a hot job there. One thing, this sun'll wilt them weeds you've hoed."

"It's wiltin' me, too. What do yuh want?"

"Thought I'd come round in the daytime when I didn't have a herd of grass-eaters pushin' me and thank yuh fer tellin' me about the campin' place and bed-ground."

"Well, yer welcome. I jest didn't want yer stock tearin' through this corn patch. Nothin' makes me madder."

"Kin I tie old Buck under that cottonwood so he can cool off? I'd like to feel a hoe handle again."

All Millie could say was, "I guess that won't hurt nothin'. I got t' go work in the house perty soon, though."

Cameron came back from the cottonwood and watched the girl hoe, the tool making soft sounds in the sandy soil.

"Here, ma'am, let me try for a spell. I never thought I'd ever ask for a hoe again. Our old place was jest rocks and grit. We wore out a hoe or two every spring."

Millie hesitated. She didn't want any man hanging around. Hot and tired, dirty and self-conscious, she was also proud, resentful of any help, and here was this smiling man reaching for the hoe, acting like she would be doing him a favor if she let him use it. His dark-brown eyes were calm as he looked at her, the gray Stetson on the back of his head, damp beads of sweat on his forehead where the sun hadn't tanned it. Suddenly she pushed the handle toward him in surrender.

Cameron began cutting weeds and mulching the soil around the plants. Slow and deliberate in contrast to the girl's swift skill, after a few minutes, he said, "I stopped in to see Jervis the other night. Seems like a nice feller. He thinks a lot of you folks."

Millie was immediately suspicious. "Well, how come yuh talked about us? Yuh had no call to do that."

"A whiskered feller I met up east told me Jervis could be trusted. When we got acquainted, I asked him about you. I figgered we might be friends."

This was logical. Maybe it was okay to talk with this man. "Mister Jervis is a friend of ours. Who was the whiskered feller?" Millie was weeding cabbage plants. Cameron was doing a better job in the corn. He went on scratching away, liking the sound and the feel of the tool in the silty soil.

"Had a pack of grub, wore a Mex hat, overalls and boots, flannel shirt, and a blue-and-red neckerchief. Denny, he said his name was. Seemed like a nice feller."

"We know him. My older brother Max works at his mine, the Ajax. My sister Lou and one o' my younger brothers went up t' see him t'day. We like Mister Denny."

Cameron looked back to the girl, turned in his direction. His heart fluttered. Her hair, red and shining in the sun, hung about her face.

"I see how anybody would. Looked honest and hard-workin'. Where do yuh want me to work now? I've finished the corn."

Trying not to feel conscious of her dusty,

sweat-streaked face, she answered, "Start on the squash and melons if yuh want, but you can't hoe too close. I'll git the weeds you miss in the vines. Where do yuh live, Mister Cameron?"

"No place in particular. BMT Cattle Company's got a thousand or so head up near Duck Lake. Know where Wells Creek is?"

"I've heerd of it. Not very big, is it?"

"Jest a place to whoop and holler. Little store, and saloon of course, and the stage stop. Ranch headquarters is four or five miles west of there."

Running from the house, Manny stopped when he saw the stranger. "Millie," he said shyly, "when I come up from the river I see Paw's fell off his chair. We gotta git him in the house."

Cameron asked, "Can I help, ma'am?"

"Yeah . . . maybe you kin, iffen yuh don't mind."

Around the corner of one hogan, lying on the hard-packed earth, was Amos Blecker, fallen face down from his chair. They heard his heavy, labored breathing. Millie tried to turn him over, but Cameron said, "Ma'am, let me do it. Tell me where yuh want him."

"In the house. Manny, hold the door open."

Millie went through the main room, with its fireplace and tables, then led Cameron with Amos in his arms, into a smaller room fashioned of woven willows backed on the outside with sod and blocks of dried mud and sand. Millie motioned Cameron to place her father on a couch made of poles and woven rawhide strips covered with soogans.

Blecker began to breathe easier. Millie opened his shirt, picked up a goosewing fan, and knelt to fan it over his face.

"Can I get a doc?"

"No, there ain't nothin' we kin do but try to cool him off. Perty quick he'll be better. Go out and set. I'll be out perty soon—we kin talk."

Out on the shaded porch, Cameron sat down, rolled a cigarette, and smoked. The boy had disappeared. Cameron studied the walls of the house, looked across to the river, and thought. He heard her dress swish as Millie pushed the cowhide door aside and stepped out.

"Mister Cameron, thanks. I'll clean up. Then would yuh eat a bite?"

"Whatever yuh say, ma'am. Don't fix anything special. I'd like to talk about your paw before I leave."

Millie washed, changed into the only other dress she had, and combed her hair. In the room that served as a kitchen, she quickly set out lunch, biscuits, baked beans warm from the fireplace, and sliced cold meat. There was water to drink.

Cameron left an hour later, having learned more about Amos Blecker, Denny and Jervis. He had his own thoughts about Millie, and he would be back.

7

CAMERON PLANS A SWAP

CAMERON LOPED HIS buckskin over to Hooper's
Bend Merchantile and found Jervis reading papers
the stage had dropped off. It was cool in the darkened back room. Cameron took a chair.

"Somethin' on yer mind, mister?" Jervis asked.

"Jest come from Bleckers'. The old man had a
spell and was plumb out when I left. Any doc seen
him about that busted head of his lately?"

Jervis rubbed and polished his reading glasses
with a white handkerchief, slipped them into a

case, and got up. As he turned, he looked at the sprawling rider.

"Sometimes I think they'd be better off without the old man," he replied. "He gives damn good advice when he comes to, and the kids keep waiting. The doc ain't seen him fer six months. Opinion I gather is that he'll gradually get worse."

"What'll happen to those kids when he kicks off?"

"Nothin' worse'n's going' on now. Maybe it'll be better. Say, how come Millie let yuh stick around? She runs every other feller to hell outa there."

"I hoed a few rows of corn and melons and she done some weedin'. Then her little brother come for her to help her old man back in the house. We ate somethin', and I come in. She never told me not to come back."

"Well, far as I know, you're the first young feller ever talked with her or was let in the house. She tell yuh about her brother Loper bein' killed?"

"Yeah. Hold-up rider shot him, she said."

"Denny and I and mebbe one or two other don't like it. Nor several things like it that've happened."

"Any objections if I deal myself in?"

"Hell, no. If yuh can help us find out about the hold-up, why not? Don't spread it around, though. Jest ridin' out t' the Bleckers' kin start stories." Jervis mused. "There's a way you could help that girl out."

"Yeah?"

"Help her trade a pair of their ornery, long-eared mules for a milk cow. Millie's been tryin', but nobody'll have the critters."

"Don't they need 'em for plowing and hauling?"

"They got another team. Lou and Kiah rode 'em up to the mine today. Maybe you can work up a deal. You look like a horse-trader."

Cameron rolled a cigarette and looked around for a match. Jervis reached to a shelf for a box of them. The cowpuncher lit up and after a few slow drags, said, "I could sell the outfit, buy a cow, and give her the extra cash. Reckon she could use that."

"She's perty proud. If she figgered you was goin' outa your way to help her, she might pull back."

Cameron continued to smoke. "Know of a good milker around here I could buy?"

"Oh, she'd find out an' see through that easy. Somethin' from up your way might be better."

Cameron purchased a few things, thanked Jervis, and rode off. Ben Jervis watched the buckskin trot north for the river crossing.

At dark, Lou and Kiah passed Hooper's Bend on their way home from the Ajax Mine, enough rocks in four gunnysacks slung over their tall mules to drown all the cats in the country. Mr. Denny had asked them to keep the stuff at home.

Millie understood. This time Mr. Denny might manage to get his gold down to the assay office without being robbed. It would be safe with the

Bleckers until he got ready to ship it.

Percy Cameron looked for a young cow, hoping to find her fairly close to Hooper's Bend. She must have a calf by her side, and be bred back. Up at Wells Creek in the valley he knew of several hayshakers squatted on an odd piece of land they plowed, planting spuds, grain and orchards in the dark, silty loam.

Otto Klinger had a big, buxom woman and a flock of kids and was interested in producing everything that would grow, starting with children who could pull weeds, feed chickens, pick potato bugs, and milk cows. Cameron stopped at Klinger's place to swap the time of day. The two men talked about crops and stock, and Cameron told Klinger about the good milk cows on his father's farm back in Illinois. When they spoke of horses, Cameron was on more familiar ground.

"Mister Klinger, you know anything about mules?"

"No, mooles I don't know. Horses, you bet."

"I saw a good team of mules the other day, big rawboned critters, so tall you'd need a stepladder to hang your hat on the hames. Those mules are the plow-pullingest, tough-haulingest, hard-workingest critters in the country."

The old German thought such a team could break his tough meadow sod. "What's wrong mit 'em, Cameron?"

"They're the farthest thing from outlaws. Been raised by a bunch of kids who can do anything with 'em, and they don't savvy growed up people too well. Maybe your kids could handle that pair."

"Ya say kids drive 'em? No trouble mit kickin'?"

"They're gentle. Jest goldarned pets that like kids around 'em. Dangest thing!"

Klinger could see the possibilities. If he owned something kids could drive he'd get more work done. "What they vant for 'em? Why they vant to sell?"

"That's the ringy part—they want to trade for a cow. They only need one team and they got two. I tried to buy the team I'm talking about for freight hauling', but they need a cow and calf, and I've got no kids to handle the critters."

"Where do these people live?"

"Over near Hooper's Bend. That's sure a team!"

"What would it take to swap?"

Cameron considered. "If you're interested, Klinger, maybe I can help yuh get ahold of that team of mules. Your kids could drive 'em, all right."

The farmer was beginning to itch. In his mind he could see the tall, slow creatures, a boy of his driving them while he held the plow steady in the sod. He could hear the plowshare rip through roots, smell the fresh dirt, and see the ribbon of sod roll back from the furrow. He could imagine neighbors marveling that his boy could handle such critters. The logs they could skid, the stumps they could pull, the freight they could haul to town! By gollies!

"Mr. Cameron, vat you think I got to trade for dem mooles? You made me deal, huh?"

"Sure, I could pick out what I think they might take in trade, but I don't want one red cent out of the deal. You're my neighbor and they're my friends. Savvy?"

"Yah, yah, I understand. Go ahead, Mister Cameron."

"Well, they've got the whole outfit, team, harness, wagon. Have yuh got a light single-horse rig, a buggy or light wagon?"

"Yah, yah, I got one. I show you."

"They'd need that in trade for theirs and a pony to go with it they can ride or drive. Their wagon ain't new but it's a good one. Fair enough?"

"Yah, yah!" But Klinger was most interested in the mules themselves.

"The team's worth two hundred bucks, clean of harness," Cameron went on. "Now if you can trade a cow, a heifer calf, a pair of shoats and a dozen chickens, you might get a deal. Yeah, and a pup from that bitch shepherd."

"She's a goot dog, all right."

"Nice if you'd keep one out for them. And Mister Klinger, I'll leave it up to you to pick the cow, one the kids can milk, not a kicker nor hard-titted. I'll be seeing the kids and their paw in a few days. If they like it, I'll send them over with the team and wagon. They'll show your kids how to handle the mules, make 'em pull and stand."

"Yah, yah, you tell 'em to come see me. I deal," said the tight-fisted German.

"There'll just be two little kids with the team—you could beat 'em in a deal, but I think you're a man of your word and I'll leave it in your hands. The trip'll take two days, so be ready to feed and sleep 'em."

"Mister Cameron, you chust trust me. I make a fair deal. I won't cheat no orphans. I see they get a goot cow, goot heifer too." He led Cameron to the barn pasture. The brown-and-white shepherd bitch darted under the rails, circling the cows and calves feeding there and then headed them for the barn.

The cow Klinger had in mind for the Bleckers was a medium-sized brown-and-white animal with short, sharply curved horns and neat hooves. Cameron recognized the breed.

"Chersey blood in her, Mister Cameron. From the islands in English Channel. A goot cow. My girls milk all the cows so your kids won't have no troubles.

"Now the pigs. I pick a sow pig and a boar pig. These pigs all colors, fattened on grass, potatoes und corn."

"Mister Klinger, I'll leave that to you. The kids'll have a hell of a long trip in this heat with the critters."

"I remember that. Now, let's go see what the woman has to eat. I tell her about the deal we chust made."

"Why thanks, Klinger, I won't turn down a meal."

"Goot!" They walked back to the house. "Ven

you think those kids will bring mooles?''

"Well, I'll see them in three days. If they leave there the next, that's four, then two for the trip. Better figger about a week from today.''

8

GOOD-BYE TO MOSE AND MAISIE

LEVI ESCH HADN'T forgotten the hold-up. He
waited, wondered what would happen next and
when, and sized up every person who entered or
left Willow Springs. In conversations around his
boardinghouse table, at the livery stable, and in
the street, he listened for bits of helpful information.

A stranger riding into town stopped at the saloon

across the road for a drink and asked a few questions. Levi watched him cross to his side of the road.

"Mister Esch?"

"I'm Levi Esch."

"Could yuh spend a little time with me someplace where we could argue awhile?" the stranger asked. Levi sized up the rider. He motioned the man to follow him to the floor above, where he opened a door, went down a short hall and in an unoccupied room showed the stranger to a chair, leaving the door open and seating himself so he could see down the hall.

"What's on your mind, mister?"

"My name's Cameron. I boss a herd of BMT cattle up near Duck Lake. Ben Jervis told me you buried a boy name of Loper Blecker got shot in a hold-up a while back, an' I met Denny, who hired the boy to take care of that box of gold the outlaws got. When I met the Blecker kids and their paw, I decided to butt in to see they got a fair shake from here on out. I ain't lookin' for trouble, Mister Esch, understand? I come here to meet yuh and let yuh know I'm keepin' an eye on what happens that concerns the people I named."

Levi's heart beat faster. This man might be the one they needed. He was frank, he looked capable of handling himself without stumbling, was old enough to be halfway smart, young enough to raise hell without counting costs.

"Mister Cameron, the Blecker family has my sympathy, but they're independent and proud, so

I've waited. What'd you want to know from me?''

"How was it Lope got killed?''

"Let me warn you right now, Mister Cameron, that you might be headin' for trouble. This country ain't too civilized—the forces behind these robberies and killings are too big for one or two men to handle.''

"If these outlaws can rob stages and kill people for their money at will, maybe they'll get big and bold enough to rob me an' my bosses. If I nip 'em in the bud, I'd really be worth my salt.''

Old Levi smiled. "Mister Cameron, I'm with you. I'll answer your questions as best I can.''

"I want to learn the name of every honest man in this part of the country and where they live. Now tell me what you know of the hold-up and what yuh think of the driver, Rufe Bledsoe.''

Levi told Cameron how the trap was set, and of the ambush at Cow Hollow. "If Bledsoe trusted you,'' he went on, "he might give you some ideas. If he's sure you mean business, he'll join you, but not until then.''

Cameron shook Esch's hand when he left the hotel, deciding they would communicate through Ben Jervis and see each other in an emergency. Back to spend the night in Hooper's Bend, Cameron saw Ben Jervis. He did not go to Flora's, but found a place to sleep undisturbed. The Bleckers would be up early. The cowboy had breakfast at the hotel.

Millie had been wondering about the buckskin's

rider and was curious and strangely excited. The memory of Cameron lay mellow on her mind. Would he come back? What had he thought of her—and her sick father? Did he really want to help her or was he just trying to get her out in the bushes? Millie Blecker was realistic. She knew why Flora Miller kept girls at her place, and who Agnes Millsap entertained in her dressmaking shop.

Cameron rode up to the Blecker settlement at seven that morning. Lou and Kiah hoed in the garden and Manny weeded melons. Millie was nowhere in sight.

"Good mornin'! Your sister around?"

"Good mornin', mister. Does she know yuh?" Lou stopped hoeing and looked across the willow fence. This must be the man who had been to see her sister while she and Kiah were at the Ajax.

"I reckon she does. I stopped here a few days ago. My name's Cameron."

"She's over t' town cleaning' house fer a lady, Mister Cameron."

"I'm sure sorry to miss her. Thought I'd get here early enough, but I see you folk're up and on the job 'fore daylight. You must be Lou, and this is Kiah. Is that Manny over there? I'll tell you all what I come for."

"Come on, boys, let's set a spell," Lou said.

They walked to the end of the garden and sat on a cottonwood log. Cameron tied his horse and loosened the cinch. He began to build a cigarette.

"Kids, Mister Jervis said you had a team of

mules an' a wagon to swap. I run into a feller name of Klinger can use 'em an' we come up with the makin's of a deal.''

"Paw told Millie t' look fer a trade. He thought we oughta git a milk cow—have our own milk an' butter, an' raise us a calf."

"Lou, this ain't an easy one-way deal. Can you kids drive those mules and plow with 'em? Could you teach a coupla other kids about your size to work 'em?''

"We could—huh, Lou?" Kiah assured, looking at his sister.

"Mister Cameron," Lou was serious, "we growed up with them mules. They won't work fer grown-ups. You cain't hit 'em, yuh gotta kinda baby 'em along. Pet 'em an' pat 'em."

"Think Klinger's kids could work 'em?"

"I kin guarantee it, iffen the kids ain't mean. Mose an' Maisie won't stand fer that."

"The kids aren't mean. The mules'll hafta work, but Klinger takes care of his stock. Now I said you'd swap your harness and the wagon for a small rig and a pony you could ride or drive and his harness. Klinger said okay. The team of mules goes for a good milk cow, a heifer calf, two pigs and a dozen chickens, and you can pick a pup from a litter his shepherd bitch has. But you kids'll hafta deliver the mules and wagon to Klinger's homestead in Duck Valley. It'll take two days and you'll hafta bring the stock and other stuff back. Can you do that?''

The three Bleckers went into conference. Who

would go? If Kiah and Lou went, who would help Mr. Jervis and work in the garden? If Manny and Lou went, would they be able to handle a cow and calf, two pigs, the chickens, and a strange pony? And could they show the Klinger kids how to handle Mose and Maisie?

The cowman listened, venturing no opinion as it was decided that Manny and Lou would go.

"I told the old man I figured you'd be there Sunday," he said. "I'd travel at night. You'll make better time and it'll be easier. I'll make yuh a map to show where you could make camp."

"Yeah—we don't know nothin' 'bout that part of the country."

"Get me a piece of paper and I'll write down the deal so there won't be no mistakes."

Lou ran for the house, her short dress whipping around her legs. Kiah and Manny watched as the tall buckeroo sketched in the dust at their feet the roads and waterholes enroute to Wells Creek.

"You cross the river here," he told the boys. "Half mile over, swing east. The road leaves the river—the next water's a crick fifteen miles on, but it's near dry except in lava holes. Travelin' about ten miles farther yuh come to a fork. A sign says Wells Creek right, an' Duck Lake left. Take the road to Duck Lake. Two miles, and you'll see a patch of aspen up to the west. There's a little seep. Camp there. Next day yuh can make it to Klingers'. You come to three or four farms 'fore his. The house an' barns're on the left under the lava wall, new orchard an' garden near the crick, and milk cows in the field below the house. He'll be lookin' for yuh.''

Lou was back with pencil and brown wrapping paper, breathing heavily from her run, her cheeks flushed with excitement. ''Mister Cameron, you certain we kin trade the mules an' wagon fer all them things?''

''Well, that's what we talked about. I'll draw the map on one side of the paper and write down the deal on the other. Have your sis sign for you and if Klinger's satisfied, he'll sign. Remember, it's no deal if the mules won't work for his kids. And make sure the pony ain't tender-footed.''

Lou was already wistful. ''I sure hope he takes good keer of Mose and Maisie.''

''On the road back, don't feed the pigs but very little and make sure yuh have water along to pour on sacks an' put over 'em in the sun. The cow's a heavy milker, so keep her bag milked out.''

''Mister Cameron,'' Lou told him, ''we're sure glad yuh made a deal fer us. Millie didn't say nothin' 'bout yer lookin' fer a deal.''

''She didn't know about it. Ben Jervis told me about the trade you wanted. Just plain luck Klinger was lookin' fer a big strong team. You kids tell your sis about it—and good luck. Your paw still in bed?''

''Yep. He don't know nothin' 'bout what's goin' on. Kiah'll stay here 'cause Millie works most of the time an' only she or Kiah's big enough t' help him.''

Cameron tightened the saddle cinch, picked up

the reins, and swung up. "Don't forget the pup," he said. "He'll keep stock outa the garden and ride herd on the cow. Keep varmints away, too. So long." Just before the river, he looked back. The Blecker kids were watching him and raised their hands in answer to his wave.

When Millie came home that evening she was astonished to see the wagon near the house, Mose and Maisie hitched to it, Kiah and Lou loading in a few things, and Manny working on a new fence down under the cottonwoods. Something was going on. When she heard what it was, she sat down in the willow chair and cried. It was too good to be true. Her thoughts whirled, but at their center something told her the Bleckers' luck had changed.

An hour later, Lou and Manny drove out of the yard. With luck, they would all be drinking milk and selling butter within a week.

9

THE TRIP TO KLINGERS' RANCH

AFTER THE WAGON'S rattle died away, Millie and her brother talked. Millie and Kiah would have to get along the next few days without help, but it was a relief to get rid of the mules and Millie had never dreamed of getting so much in return.

"Kiah, yuh think the Klinger kids kin work them mules?"

"Mister Cameron told Mister Klinger the deal wouldn't be no good lessen his kids could handle Mose and Maisie fair an' square."

Now it was cool and a little breeze came up the river, stirring leaves on the cottonwood and cooling the hot sand.

"Say, Kiah, what do yuh think of Mister Cameron?"

"He's all right, a lot better'n some cowboy buckeroos. He wanted t' see yuh, but when yuh wasn't here he laid out the deal an' rode off. Said he'd drop in first chance he had t' see how the farm was comin' along."

When Millie went to bed she thought for a few minutes of the tall cowboy, and of her brother and sister driving the mule team across sagebrush flats on the way to Klingers'. Then she slept, too tired to dream.

The old mules splashed across the shallow river, ground their way up through gravel and rocks and came to the dusty road. When they felt a touch of the willow switch and a flap of the reins they broke into a long, swinging trot. The wagon wheels, tight in their iron rims from standing in the river, rolled along, rattling as they moved on the axles.

The full moon came up over ragged rims to the southeast. In the warm night they heard nighthawks swoop and boom, smelled sand, drying sagebrush and the tang of juniper. Gritty dust clung to the mules' nostrils and occasionally one sneezed.

They watered at a crossing, the lava rock black and shining in the moonlight. Lou got out to stretch her legs, then washed her dusty hands and face in a pool. They were making good time. The moon had swung around to the southwest. It was almost morning.

Klinger, back of the barn, heard his kids yelling. "Pa . . . Pa . . . the kids an' their mules're comin'!"

Excited, Klinger rounded the corner and looked down the lane as a team of mules and a canvas-topped wagon entered it and approached his buildings. Why, they were a day early!

Lou took charge, introduced herself and Manny. "Mister Klinger, which of yer young-uns're goin' t' drive the mules?" she asked.

"Miss Louisiana, vy you ask that?"

"If yuh show me which ones, I kin start gettin' the mules acquainted. The critter're tired an' thirsty. If yer kids unharness 'em, and lead 'em t' water, let 'em roll and feed 'em, them mules'll know they're among friends."

"Vell now, sure. You kids settle it. You chust go ahead, Miss Lou. I stand back und vatch you."

Lou handed the reins to her brother, clambered down over the wagon wheel, and walked to one of the girls. "I'm Lou, what's yer name?"

"Truda. At school they call me Trudy."

"Well, Trudy, rub yer hands on me where I been sweatin' so yuh'll smell like me. That way they'll know we been close together. There, that'll do. Don't be afraid of 'em. We raised 'em from little colts an' they won't bite er kick if yer careful. Jest watch yer feet when yuh stand along side of 'em."

Lou went to the mules' heads and one reached down to nudge her shoulder. "This here's Mose,

wants me to take off his harness." Lou took
Trudy's hand and let Mose sniff it. "Rub his ears
an' loosen the bridle." Mose lowered his head
and, standing on tiptoe, Trudy rubbed his long
velvety ears.

"This here's Maisie, a mare mule. She's the
boss." Maisie sniffed the girls and waited for attention. "Baby 'em all yuh kin," Lou went on,
"but when they start gittin' smart jest switch 'em
an' scold 'em. Now which boy wants t' help yuh?"

Bashful Klaus, about thirteen, stood up near the
wagon, tall beside Manny.

"Manny, show Klaus how t' git acquainted,"
Lou told her brother.

Otto Klinger, his wife, and the rest of the family
watched in amazement. The Klinger kids entered
into the spirit of the introductions. Manny crawled
over and under the mules, had them lower their
heads and lift their feet, looked into their mouths.
Klaus gained confidence, and when Lou called to
the team to follow, mules and children walked
together to the barn, the wagon rolling behind
them.

Under Lou's watchful eye, Klaus and his sister
unharnessed the team, put on halters and led them
to the water trough. Then the kids climbed on the
mules, Lou with Trudy, Manny behind Klaus, and
rode to the end of the lane and back. In the corral
they were turned loose to roll in the dust. Otto
Klinger gloated over his team. He saw what Cameron meant by their value.

Lou and Manny, shy about eating in another
house, hardly knew what to do when Mrs. Klinger

put helping after helping on their plates. Orphans they were; all her mother love brimmed over.

Next morning Trudy took Lou and Manny to see the cows and milk little brown Jersey. For the Klingers she was gentle and an easy milker but Lou and Manny had to bend their fingers hard and squeeze. Trudy laughed. Practice would make it easy, she said.

Trudy and Klaus had fed Mose and Maisie, and now they led the team out to where their harness lay in the wagon. Klaus slipped the collar around Mose's neck, standing on a block to buckle it. While Mose stood watching, Trudy held the breeching, and they snapped and buckled it. Mose lowered his head for bridle and bit. Then it was Maisie's turn.

Manny directed the harnessing of the team while Lou talked to Otto. "Mister Klinger, them mules er too big t' push around," she told him. "Yuh cain't beat 'em, either. Sometime yuh might want t' light a fire under 'em or skin 'em alive if they balk and jest stand and look at yuh. Then's when yuh gotta git somethin' they like, an' talk to 'em. They won't fight yuh. Yuh don't hafta worry about that. All yuh hafta do is figure out how t' hit 'em t' do things the way yuh want and let the kids take over."

Klinger knew this serious, freckle-faced girl was talking sense. The mules liked to be patted and coddled; now if they'd just work for the Klingers everything would be fine. There was that log he wanted to skid to the house, already chained and hooked to the doubletrees. Manny took over.

"Klaus, you take them lines, an' Trudy, you git ahead where they kin see yuh. If they don't move fer Klaus, pick up some grass and show it to 'em and tell 'em to come an' git it. Are yuh ready?"

"Mose! Maisie! Giddap!" Klaus shook the long leather lines. The mules leaned forward, felt the weight of the log, and began to walk. Trudy headed for the barn and the team followed right along.

An hour later, Klinger knew he had a team that would be of great help in homesteading this land. His kids could do anything with them. While they worked, Lou told Otto what the mules liked, how to work them in his garden, and keep them from being nuisances.

Klinger displayed the pony mare he had picked for the wagon. They chose pigs and hens, admired and talked about the cow and calf. Klinger filled a sack with corn for the trip home. They loaded the wagon, and by six o'clock that night Lou and Manny and their stock were ready to leave.

It was hot when they pulled out. Nelly, the Jersey cow, was broke to lead and her heifer calf stepped along beside her.

When the sun dropped over the hills in the west it began to cool down, but by the time they reached the camp ground at the aspen grove they were ready to stop.

They unhitched the pony and let her loose on a rope to roll and feed. The cow and calf grazed a little, then lay down. After they had slept a little while, the two kids harnessed up. Cow and calf tied behind, they headed for Hooper's Bend.

The stock was weary when they came to the

creek crossing the lava rock and made camp. It was hot, the sun three hours high, but they were less than twenty miles from home and they would make it that night. They milked the cow, watered the pigs, staked out their horse, and fed the chickens. There were eggs and milk for breakfast.

They lay in the shade the rest of that hot day while the stock fought flies, fed on sparse grass, and rested. The pigs grunted and moaned in their crates but quieted down when a pail of water was splashed over them. The chickens held their wings away from their bodies, their bills open. The heat didn't bother Rascal, the shepherd pup. Full of mischief and play, he rolled and tumbled, licked the kids' faces, barked at the horse, jumped in the creek, chased grasshoppers and finally, worn out, slept cuddled in Manny's arm.

They waited until seven o'clock that evening. The sun had dropped almost to the horizon when they drove out to the dusty road. Before morning they would be home, even if they had to stop to rest the stock. They had finished the hard part of the trip.

The two miles before they reached the river crossing were the worst. It was still dark. The calf gave out and lay down, the cow was footsore and weary, the kids sleepy—and the pup was full of plain old hell.

Many twisted the calf's tail. No use. He held its nose. It jerked away and closed its eyes. Lou lowered the wagon's endgate and by sheer strength and will power they got the calf's front feet up to the wagon bed, lifted and heaved. The calf was loaded.

Wading the shallow river revived the pony and cow. The freshness of the green foliage and the smell of grass and water gave them new life. They turned into the Blecker place and stopped. The journey was over.

Millie heard the wagon and called Kiah. The kids had brought home unbelievable riches: a good harness, too, and what a cow! It was easy to see she was a real milk cow. And the big, smooth heifer calf, pigs squealing in crates and a wiggling, tongue-licking, rolling-on-ground puppy!

"Millie, we got eggs fer breakfast! The cow milks easy! Mr. Klinger give us feed fer the chickens an' pigs. Ain't it wonderful? We brung things from Mrs. Klinger—plants an' jelly an' seeds." Lou and Manny talked a blue streak at once while they unharnessed the pony. They tied the calf down by the garden, left the cow to rest right where she was, and let out the pigs and chickens.

Dawn was breaking when they went into the house. Millie got breakfast. If ever she felt like dropping to her knees and thanking the Lord, it was right then. The Bleckers had their own stock; they were beholden to no one. Mr. Cameron had something special to do with this trade—why had he made it possible? Well, she would have to thank him and find that out later.

10

IN LOST RIVER COUNTRY

BEN JERVIS WAS floored when Millie came in to buy a churn. She paid cash and wanted to know if she could trade butter and eggs for other things. Astounded and curious, he learned they had traded mules and wagon for a cow and calf, two pigs, a dozen hens, a cayuse and a light wagon. He just couldn't quite bring himself to believe it until Millie told him Cameron had made the deal with an old German farmer up on Duck Lake Meadows.

Jervis thought Cameron must have paid the farmer some boot. Everyone around Hooper's Bend knew those mules—why, nobody but the Blecker kids could handle them. That old German hayshaker would give Cameron a taste of buckshot if he ever went back.

Mr. Denny and Max gophered deeper into mountain rock, now so used to each other that they acted like partners, no thought given to any special working hours. In the mine, everything had to be done by candlelight. When they wheeled the barrow out in the daylight to search for high-grade ore, Max knew what to look for and how to heft rock for possible value.

Old Man Denny began to figure how he could get the gold he'd sent on the mules with the Blecker kids to the assay office without being waylaid en-route. From their place to the town where it could be assayed and sold was over a hundred miles— four days by a team of mules and a heavy wagon. The less time on the road the better. He must find a way to send the high-grade so outlaws who might be on the watch wouldn't be suspicious. If the Bleckers headed south with their big team and wagon, somebody would wonder why. It was common knowledge that Denny spent all summer digging in his mine, and anybody'd realize he'd eventually make a trip out to cash in his gold and get money. Nope, there would have to be a better plan.

The town was quiet. Cameron knew he could find excitement at Flora's but he didn't want to go there. He decided to bed down above the river and ride to the Blecker's early the next morning to be sure of seeing Millie. He could eat in town later.

Lou and Kiah, going out to milk the cow and feed the pigs, heard the pony nicker, and looked up to see Cameron riding the buckskin down the riverbank. They raised their voices as one, "Millie, here comes Mister Cameron!"

The rider heard their call and raised a palm in welcome. Millie came to the doorway, turned back in haste to give her hair a quick combing and tied a ribbon around it. She smoothed her dress and went outside, her bare feet making no sound on the sandy soil.

"Why, good mornin', ma'am, I got here early enough this time."

"Mister Cameron, we got eggs, milk, cream, an' our own butter fer breakfast. Better plan on eatin' with us. Yuh own a share of the food."

"Don't see how you figger that, ma'am. But if you don't mind cookin' for a lost cowpuncher, I'll sure stay. I come around to see what the kids brought back."

"A sight more'n I expected. Lou said old man Klinger was tickled with the trade."

"Could the Klinger kids work the mules?"

"Took to 'em like Lou and Kiah took to the new pup."

"Well, I'm sure glad of that." Cameron's smile was warm and his eyes held hers until Lou broke in.

"Mister Cameron, I done learned to milk our cow." The story of the trip was told, how the kids made friends with the Klingers, how the mules worked for Trudy and Klaus, their leavetaking, and the difficulties of the hot trip home. Millie went in the house to get breakfast ready. This time she would have real coffee.

Cameron stayed for more than two hours. Eating breakfast in the house that was a conglomeration of hogans, he saw that the Bleckers lived on the edge of real poverty. The dishes were an assortment of tin containers, the tin cutlery scarce and of odd sizes. There were only two chinaware cups. Cooking was done over a raised fireplace, Mexican style. They had made all their furniture from scrap wood and willow. There would be more to eat now, though, and the cowman knew there were hundreds of other settlers not much better off in this country.

Lou and Manny made comparisons to the Klingers, who ate at a table covered with a cloth, every plate chinaware, all the service dishes full of food. Mrs. Klinger served white bread, they said, and there was a silver knife, fork and spoon at every place. The Klingers were rich.

Ever since Cameron had entered their lives, the Bleckers had talked about him, speculating about the company he worked for, estimating him as a friend. Max was away, Loper was dead. Heavy responsibility rested on Millie, and she tried to share it with Lou and Kiah, but they all knew now that if Cameron was around they could ask him for advice.

It was Millie's dressmaking day. Kiah hooked up the pony and drove her to town. Cameron rode alongside. Townspeople up and at work saw the

Blecker kids and the cowman. The story of Bleckers swapping the mule team and wagon for a lot of livestock and a light wagon had spread all over the little valley. The general feeling was that "Them Bleckers pulled a fast one. Everybody knows them danged mules're no good."

Ben Jervis swept out the front of his store, using oiled sawdust to keep down the dust, and whistled a tuneless song. Cameron clomped across the porch. "Well, if it ain't Mister Cameron," Jervis greeted. "Figgered you to be up to Duck Lake with the cows."

"Naw, we're moving a bunch of bulls from lake country up to the meadow winterin' grounds. I come down to see how the Blecker kids made out. Got time to put up some tobacco and a few other things?"

"Sure, that's what I'm here for. Say, yuh musta made a hell of a deal with somebody. The kids brought back more plunder than a tribe of Modocs. Who'd yuh stick with those outlaw mules?"

"Never stuck nobody. The feller got 'em is tickled pink."

"Is that right! What makes him so happy? Yuh didn't give no boot, did yuh?"

"Didn't have to. Ever figger why those long-ears wouldn't work for a muleskinner?"

"Nope. Why?"

"Hell, muleskinners beller, pop their cracker, and cuss. Those mules were brought up as pets by a bunch of little kids. That was the trick in the deal. The feller that got 'em lets his kids drive 'em. That's all the critters need. I'll bet yuh couldn't

91

buy them mules off him for love nor money.''

"Well, I'll be damned! What kind of tobacco yuh want?''

Half an hour later, Cameron and his buckskin single-footed north out of town. He only glanced toward the Blecker place. He was on the way to the new bulls and his winter home at Duck Lake meadows. Summer would soon turn to fall; he had much to do. But he would come this way again before long and start digging into a few things. Maybe he'd learn something he wanted to know.

11

JOURNEY WITH GOLD

MANNY AND KIAH BLECKER came riding into the Ajax camp on the bay pony. They had brought supplies, and a story of the fantastic deal they'd made trading the mules.

Coming out of the hole, Max and the old miner cleaned up at the spring, and marveled at their good luck and Cameron's part in it all. Denny was pleased that his chance meeting with the cowman on the buckskin had led to this.

His mind once more on the problem of getting a shipment of gold to the assay office, Denny began tying details together. With the accumulation of ore at the Bleckers' and another fifty pounds of good stuff they would dig out after the next shot, he could have the assay office hold part of it, and get an advance to take care of him and Max for several months.

If Max and Kiah left in the dark, traveled through Willow Springs, then pulled off the road and slept during the day, they had a good chance of not being stopped. Maybe nobody would think a couple of kids and their pony had anything valuable.

During long hot days, he decided he and Max would work another shot, take out the hot stuff. Then Max could make a trip home with more specimens, he and Kiah would harness the pony, load in all the ore, and head for Virginia City.

The shot was a disappointment; they found the vein pinching out. Max wheeled a few loads into the light and Denny examined their meager take. "Boy," he said finally, "let's try to change our luck. You take off for Hooper's Bend, get a few of your sister's meals under your belt, then you and Kiah haul the ore. I'll stick here and try to find where that darn vein went. You've got to figger a week er more fer the trip. Say ten days. I'll look fer yuh in about two weeks."

Max washed up, hoisted his sack of ore, and hit the trail, arriving at the Blecker place in darkness, tired and hungry. The Blecker kids sat up late to talk and plan. Millie made a list. The boys must buy shoes and clothes for everybody so this winter's cold wouldn't worry them like others they'd known.

Max stayed closed to home all of the next day. He worked on the barn Kiah and Manny had started, admired pigs and chickens, petted the pup and milked the cow. Looking over the wagon, he found a loose tire, checked the pony's feet and noticed a piece broken out of one hoof.

Kiah took the pony and wagon to the blacksmith to have the tire reset and the pony shod. Lou went with him to buy supplies at Jervis's store, both careful not to mention to anyone that Max was home or that gold ore was to be hauled to Virginia City next day.

The smith was busy in his smoky shop, shoeing a stage team. He tried to put off Kiah's jobs, but Kiah stayed at the smithy, pumping bellows and holding horses' heads, saying little, asking nothing, until his turn came. By dusk the work was done and the wagon loaded at the store; the pony's new shoes rang on the stones as she trotted home.

That night they placed sacks of ore in the wagon bed along with grain for the pony and grub boxes close to the seat, covered with canvas near a couple of soogans for their bed. When everything was loaded, Max brought out the shotgun and Amos Blecker's army revolver and hid them in the wagon bed. Kiah drove as they circled Hooper's Bend and headed south under a dark, starlit sky. Dogs yapped at the wagon's rattle. On the main road, the pony trotted easily, a cayuse bred in sage country from Spanish and Indian stock, who could keep her pace all night.

"Kiah, if we git jumped by them outlaws I ain't gonna do like Loper did," Max said. "The double barr'l's loaded with buck an' the Remington's full. If I'm drivin' an' anybody comes alongside, slip me the little gun, then lay back with the shotgun under the canvas. Keep it cocked. Yuh gotta be keerful—she goes off easy—but if I shoot, turn her loose next."

"Max, yuh figger somebody might hold us up?"

"Boy, we're haulin' gold. Loper figgered he'd bluff 'em, but he got killed. That ain't gonna happen t' us. Maybe the same fellers'll hold us up. Iffen they do, I'm gonna git me one of 'em at least. You got that shotgun."

"I'll use it, Max."

"Mister Denny said bandits allus git away 'cause they know what they're gonna do, but the fellers they're robbin' don't."

"Does Mister Denny know who them robbers were?"

"Nope. Least he didn't tell me. He's so int'rested in gopherin' he fergits other things. He cain't even sleep till he figgers what made that vein pinch out."

Through Willow Springs, they quieted and slowed the pony. As far as they could tell, no one was up in the town. A little after dawn, the boys saw trees growing thick and tall in a long row along a stream. They pulled off the road and made camp, letting the pony graze while they slept.

During their second night on the road, Max heard a horse coming from behind. He reached around and shook Kiah awake. "Rider comin'," he said. "Give me the gun, quick. Cock the double barr'l an' lay quiet."

In the dark the horseman came up along the wagon. "How fur t' the next town, stranger?"

"Dogged if I know, mister. Maybe thirty mile."

"Night's a helluva time t' travel. Where yuh from?"

"East o' Willer Springs."

In the silence, the pony snorted. The shadowy rider pulled rein. "Well . . . long road ahead." He loped away.

Kiah straightened up. "Max, that feller coulda been a spy."

"Aaaah, I dunno. . . . Could be a feller headed fer the doc er somethin'."

"His horse had been runnin' quite a spell."

"You stick outa sight. We'll camp when it's light. Two more nights t' go."

By morning, they were in high country, crossing a pass. Lava walls rose on both sides of the valley, a reddish weed painted the hills where grass was brown and dry. They saw mule deer and antelope. The road dipped southeast toward a great alkali flat, shining like snow.

Descending the grade, Max kept his eyes open for green spots. He saw aspens in a cleft a half mile west of the road and turned the pony. A seep kept the trees lush and green and the hole they dug with their shovel soon filled with sweet water. They made camp, rested, and in evening's cool put their gear in the wagon, hitched up the pony, and drove out.

On this third night, the pony heard riders coming first. She lifted her head and nickered softly. Kiah slipped down from the seat. Beneath the canvas, he handed the revolver to his brother, got the shotgun out, and cocked it. Somewhere ahead, trotting horses drew closer.

"Ho there, where yuh headed?" The call came from a man in the lead, more shadowy forms visible in the darkness behind him and to the side.

Max pulled in the pony. "Headed fer the city, mister."

"Where'd yuh camp last?"

"This side of the pass."

"See any cattle up that way?"

"We ain't seen nothin' but antelope an' deer. You lose some cattle?"

"Some feller shot and butchered a yearlin' heifer o' mine."

"Well, I ain't seen man nor critter fer forty miles."

The men stayed back, forming a widening circle.

"Sure o' that, are yuh? Maybe yuh better git down outa there an' let us take a look at yer rig."

"You the sheriff er somethin'?"

"I'm lookin' fer a load o' meat that might be hid in that rig. Git down, now!"

Surrounded, Max knew the next move was his. Like his dead brother, he had no chance to save the gold, but he wouldn't give in easy. He raised his father's revolver and fired at the shadows beyond the pony's head. Answering flashes blinded him but he pulled the trigger again and again. The pony reared. Everything around and within him exploded, and he fell into darkness.

A shotgun roared. Horses plunged, a man screamed, dying, blood choking his throat. The pony ran and crashed into a horse. Kiah heard a man shout, "Shoot the sonofabitch in the wagon!"

Trying desperately to reload, he saw a rider lean above him. The flare of burning powder was the last thing he knew.

In Hooper's Bend the Bleckers checked off the days. The boys had left Wednesday night; they should make Virginia City by Saturday. The next Monday and Tuesday would be spent at the assay office and in buying from Millie's list before starting back on Wednesday. They might make it home by the following Saturday.

That Saturday and the long hours of Sunday passed. Monday Millie went to work and Lou and Manny looked in vain for the pony and the boys. Tuesday the pigs got out and they were busy until dark rounding them up and rebuilding the pen. No one slept well Tuesday night. Wednesday was Millie's dressmaking day. Lou went to help Mrs. Ornbaw with her canning. Manny stayed home and worked in the garden.

A wind came up. Thursday noon, thunderheads formed and about three o'clock the first stroke of lightning hit Johnson's barn and set it afire. Townspeople ran to help. Another strike hit Post's outhouse. Then came rain that poured down for an hour, soaked the cut hay, wet streets, and watered gardens.

The roar of thunder, the bright flashes of lightning, brought Cap'n Amos out of bed, thinking he was at battle in the faraway south. He yelled orders, cursed, and trying to lead an attack fell over raving at the generals' stupidity. Manny covered him up and when Lou came in they got him back on the bed.

The Bleckers ate their supper, then sat under the shelter in the cool twilight. Quail called along the river, a small flight of mallards whipped up the valley, but the children's minds could not be at peace. The boys were long overdue. They worried. By Friday night Millie was sure something had happened to them.

Riding old Jack, Lou took a lunch and left at daybreak to tell Mr. Denny the boys had not returned. Millie walked to the store to see Ben Jervis.

"What can I do for you, Millie?"

"Max and Kiah left a week ago Wednesday evenin' t' take some o' Mister Denny's high-grade to Virginia City. We ain't heerd a thing from 'em. I'm afraid . . . worried 'bout 'em. What kin we do?"

Jervis thought. This was a fix. There was that old man up in the hills. "Millie, we should go over an' tell the sheriff. Too bad it's so long—tracks'll be hard to find."

Dyer listened impatiently to Millie's story. *Hell,* he thought, *that old coot Bill Denny, tryin' t' slip out some rock by hisself. Serves the old bastard right!*

"Well, best I kin do is start lookin' fer 'em," he said curtly. He rose from his desk, the conversation closed. Millie went home and cried. Things looked hopeless.

12

THE SEARCH

DENNY HEARD THE clop of heavy steps on the trail below. When he looked, he saw a gray mule, Lou Blecker on its back. The old miner knew at once that something had gone wrong. In the cabin, he set the coffee pot on the stove and chucked up the fire.

"Mister Denny!" Lou called. He was at the door. "The boys never come back, an' we ain't heard a word."

"I'm glad you're here, Lou. Get down, and set a spell."

Lou dropped rein. "Millie sent me. She went t' see Mr. Jervis." She was close to tears.

Denny looked across the sun-warmed valley. "Lou, let's go in and have some coffee. Don't give up hope. Mebbe things'll turn out all right yet."

As Lou gave him details of the boys' plans for the trip, he listened, and one thought beat in his brain. *Who in holy hell could have tipped hold-up men off to the gold cargo?* "Lou," he asked, "what did the boys do the day before they left?"

"Max stayed home, helped Manny work on the barn. Kiah took the wagon t' the smith's t' shrink a loose hind tire an' have shoes put on the pony. I went with 'em an' bought things at the store fer the boys t' take along."

"Anybody come to your place that day?"

"No. I never said nothin' t' Mr. Jervis. Kiah tol' the blacksmith he might hafta make a trip t' the valley, he didn't say where."

"When did the boys leave?"

"After dark. They was goin' t' drive south o' town, I know that, an' camp off the road in the day. Travel jest at night."

It was the way he had planned. But where had things gone wrong? Before they got to the assay office or on the way back? He'd have to trace the whole route. No one else could be trusted.

"Lou, we'll head back for your place. Can yuh put me up there for the night while I figger out what to do?"

"We'd be 'bliged." She was crying but the old man soothed her. "Mebbe they'll be there when we get there."

Lou rode old Jack and Denny walked ahead, carrying ten pounds of rich gold ore. Millie cried when she greeted him and Lou and Manny cried too. Denny tried comforting them, then waited.

Millie wiped her eyes. Beans were warming in an earthern pot by the fireplace and she set them out for supper.

On the way down, Denny had made up his mind. He had his Navy Colt revolver and a packsack to carry his gold and some grub. He would walk the trail to Virginia City and find out. Somewhere along that road the boys had met with trouble. A man on horseback might miss the signs but a man on foot could pick up clues if his eyes were keen.

"I wish Mister Cameron would ride in," Millie said. "He'd help us, I reckon; know what t' do."

Denny turned. "Do you know where Cameron is?"

"Three weeks back he left here headed fer Duck Lake. Reckon he's there," Lou said.

Denny considered this. "Has the stage gone by yet?"

"Ain't here yet. Usually comes a little later."

"Lou, can yuh run out and give Bledsoe a message for Cameron? Write something that'll fetch him in a hurry and not let nobody else know. Say, 'Death in family, come at once.' You sign it too, Millie. If he's interested in you folks he'll have that buckskin on the trail two minutes after he reads the note."

The girls wrote out their message on a piece of brown paper and signed it, "Millie and Lou, your friends." Lou scrambled up and left the house. A little later, Rufe Bledsoe saw her standing beside the road, hand held high. He stopped the team, leaned over, and asked, "What's up, Miss Louisiana?"

"This here's a messge for Mister Cameron of the BMT Cattle Company over t' Duck Lake. Will yuh see he gits it? It's mighty important. I'll pay yuh."

"Reach up aways, Lou. Yeah, he'll have it the day after t'morrow if I ketch him at Wells Crick. Don't worry 'bout no pay."

She stepped back. Rufe cracked his whip and cried, "Hi, yuh!" The stage rolled away and Lou walked slowly back to the house.

Rufus Bledsoe had already heard Sheriff Dyer was looking for two boys overdue on a trip to Virginia City and figured the Blecker boys had been hauling some of Denny's ore, had been held up and probably killed, same as their brother. He was surprised to see Cameron waiting for the stage at Wells Creek. A passenger crawled out and walked over to the cowman.

"Percy, I see you got my message," he said.

Still on his high seat, Bledsoe took the folded piece of brown paper from his pocket and called, "Mister Cameron, I got a letter fer yuh!"

Cameron opened it. "Mister Blake," he said to the arriving passenger, "may I have a word with the driver?"

"Take your time. I'll get my bag."

Cameron stepped close. "You know anything about this, Bledsoe?"

"Yer a friend o' theirs, I take it?"

"Yeah. I wanta see they get a fair shake. Levi Esch said I could trust you."

"Well, if old Levi said that, I'll level with yuh. I b'lieve their kid brothers is dead. They tried t' haul Denny's high-grade to Virginia City. Left the night of the eighth and ain't been heard of since."

"Anything on the grapevine?"

"There musta been trouble down that way. A doc in Dayton worked on a buckshot victim. Feller said some old coot let him have it when he come t' see his daughter one night. I reckon if yuh looked around yuh might hear somethin' about somebody turnin' up missin', too."

"Where would I start?"

"East slope of the pass. When I come through there early one mornin', hosses slowed down and snorted, acted kinda funny comin' along where the road narrers into lava rock. Coulda been blood spilled. If yuh want t' git down t' brass tacks, let Levi know."

"Thanks, Bledsoe. Feller got off is my boss, Rod Blake. If I come up missin', talk to him—only him. I'm leavin' in an hour. If I have a message, I'll flag yuh down."

Blake was astonished. He listened, nodding his head. When his foreman finished, he said, "I agree, Cameron we'll handle things here while you're away. Dig into this. If you need any help, let me know. You'll need the best of luck in what you may be up against."

Cameron mounted the buckskin and headed for Hooper's Bend. As he rode, he mentally checked distances, tried to form an imaginary map of country through which the boys had traveled. If they drove at night, were held up, and a fight took place, evidence of some sort might remain. And the man the doc had plucked buckshot out of seemed a good tip-off. Maybe somebody else was dead someplace.

Millie was awakened by Rascal's barking. She heard a horse's exhausted breathing, got up, pulled a dress over her head and lit the lamp. In the still night, she could hear sounds of a horse's saddle being stripped off. Barefooted, she walked to the back door. "Mister Cameron?"

"Yeah—that you, Millie?"

"Oh . . . Mister Cameron. Thank yuh fer comin'. Yuh got our message."

"That death in the family . . . Bledsoe told me about the boys bein' gone and the sheriff on the job. Don't bother to bring the light, Millie. Got an old sack I could rub Buck down with?"

Millie ran to the pigpen and came back with two grain sacks. Buck stood, head low, quivering all over, wet with sweat. As they rubbed the tired animal, Cameron on one side, the girl on the other, Millie told him about Mr. Denny's plan for the gold delivery, how the boys had left in the night. When they didn't return on time, she saw Mr. Jervis and the sheriff, sent Lou for Mr. Denny, who had already set out to look for them in his own fashion.

"Millie, if old Denny walks the whole route, you can bet those blue gimlet eyes of his'll pick up something. When did he leave?"

"Yesterday mornin'."

"I reckon Denny'll cover in daylight as much as the boys did overnight. This old pony's beginning to dry off. Don't want him to get stiff in the joints."

Millie walked beside the tall man leading Buck in the dim light of a waning moon. "Mister Cameron, nobody's come t' talk t' us. We ain't never made friends here. White trash, I reckon they call us. We ain't heerd nothin' an' I ain't been away from here since last Friday. So I cain't give yuh a steer."

They walked a moment or two in silence. "Don't let what folks think bother yuh, girl. I know it will, but like the seven plagues of Egypt, things'll pass. Let's figger our next move. Yuh got enough cash to take care of you for a spell?"

"I have some hid away here. Max was t' git paid when he cashed the gold in Virginia City. I gave him an order to fill. I swap butter and eggs fer things at the store."

Cameron took a deep breath. "Old Buck wants to lay down and roll. Got anything for breakfast? Mornin' star says daylight'll be here before long."

"Mister Cameron," Millie went on, "yuh cain't know what it means t' me t' talk. I cried . . . got that outa my system. Now it's good to be with somebody."

"Reckon I know how yuh feel. I run off from home when I was youngun—wanted to be a cowpoke. Met an old coot trapping wolves on the Yellowstone River and we shantied up for the winter. One day my partner got caught in one of his own sets, using two traps for a smart old loafer. He never come in, and when I went to look for him I found him froze stiff. He couldn't write but know-in' he was a goner he'd drawed me a picture with the hand he had loose—tried to let me see how he felt. I never quite figgered it out, except that he wasn't worried. I lived alone there for two months. If yuh want to cry, cry on my shoulder. I reckon it was made for that."

13

A HIDEOUS DISCOVERY

OLD MAN DENNY walked to Willow Springs,
stopped there to talk with Levi Esch and to eat.
Flossie brought him corned beef and cabbage, hot
bread fresh from the oven, and black coffee. Af-
terwards, the two men went upstairs. Sure now
that the Blecker boys and their pony had passed
through Willow Springs, Levi said he'd heard
rumors of trouble close to the pass, the other side
of the state line, and encouraged Denny to follow
the trail.

Denny walked. The stage passed him. He met people going to town, made his way through a herd of cattle. After the road climbed, he saw a place to make camp off the road. Sure enough, he found wagon tracks, the thin tire marks of a light rig pulled by a shod pony. There had been a camp, but no fire. The pony had grazed. Denny slept there.

Next morning the sun was on the left, then in his face. As it slipped behind his shoulder, he saw aspens ahead off the road to the right, a second good camping place for travelers. Tracks of the pony and rig were plain, headed for the aspen in the lava cleft. A dug hole filled with water. A bedded-down spot. The boys had camped here.

Tuesday morning the sun came up in a murky sky. Denny thought he might find more this day than wagon and pony tracks in dried grass and sagebrush. He had reached Nevada territory on the east side of the pass, an area not under Sheriff Dyer's jurisdiction.

A day behind the old miner, Cameron traveled at his own gait. He and Buck eased along. At Willow Springs Cameron brushed his pony down in Levi's stable while Buck ate grain and timothy hay sweet from the meadows, with clover mixed in.

In the boardinghouse diningroom, Cameron ate the baked heart and dressing Flossie brought. Levi Esch came in and sat down near him. Had Denny come that way? Levi said he had, and that they'd probably find what they were looking for east of the state line.

While they were alone, Cameron told Esch about the rumors Rufe Bledsoe had heard. An hour later he and the buckskin were on their way south.

Cameron rode until he could no longer see, then made a dry camp, Buck hobbled and left to graze while his rider rolled into his blanket, head pillowed on the saddle. When a pre-dawn breeze sprang up the next morning with Orion still hanging brightly in the sky, Cameron whistled for Buck. Cameron saddled him and rode off without eating.

Buck trotted without urging. The light grew better and Cameron watched the roadsides. He reached the second camp just after noon, and read the signs. He watered Buck, ate what he had, and went on.

At a spot in the road he thought something had taken place some time back. Rain had pattered down and a man wearing heavy boots with hobs on the edges had walked here and there. Cameron had followed those boot tracks for more than seventy miles. Denny had stopped here. This was the place.

Cameron dismounted, dropped rein. Old signs off the road still told their story: sand disturbed where shod horses had jumped and whirled, broken sagebrush; light wagon tracks and those of a pony. Had somebody tried to cover these signs over by dragging brush across the ground?

Cameron mounted Buck and tried to trail from the saddle. Half a mile away the tracks were plain. Here the rig had stopped. There were milling tracks of other horse. The trail swung north and headed for a narrow canyon between two rounded buttes.

As Cameron entered the dry wash he loosened his gun in its holster. He caught regular glimpses of Denny's boot tracks. When he rounded the butte he saw Denny squatted in the dry gulch.

Denny saw the rider approaching and stood up. "Cameron, we meet again."

"Yeah, and the circumstances ain't happy. Millie said the note Bledsoe brought me was your idea."

"I figgered you'd want in. The Blecker kids have faith in you and they need more'n an old coot like me. I tried to cheer 'em up, though."

"They trust you, too. Don't forget that. So far, I expect you know more about what happened to the boys than I do. Bring me up to date."

"I take it yuh found their camps and saw signs left in the road. Now I figger the boys got stopped, put up a scrap. I reckon they killed one or two of the skunks there in the road and got killed doin' it. Three horses were led away from where six riders stopped the boys. Up here, somebody laid and bled."

While Denny led, watching the ground, Cameron followed on Buck, thinking of the ambush. Up the gully, the trail grew narrower, barely wide enough for the rig that had still been pulled by the horse whose track they followed. Now it widened, and the way opened into a basin, its slope gentle to the top of the bench where the rig had turned east. Its track was plain to see in heavy grass and sage.

They skirted lava rimrock on the right, and far away could see the shimmer of a lake they knew was Triangle, its alkali flats white in the sun. Suddenly Denny stopped, and pointed down over the rim. Cameron got down and came to look.

"The rig went over, the boys in it, I'll bet."

They walked to look down and over. A flock of startled buzzards rose from below. "Maybe they shot the mare and rolled her over at the same time," Cameron went on. He pointed to a great blotch of blood on the grass bent flat with weight in the direction of the cliff's edge.

"I think you're right, Cameron. We gotta find a way down there, and figger out where the bandits headed too. It's getting late. S'pose I get down there, and you trail the tracks far as yuh can. If yuh come back and want me, fire once. If I come back up, I'll leave a sign, and if I head for the road without coming up I'll leave this rag on the bush by the white boulder. See the one I mean?"

Cameron nodded. "Yeah. Well, old-timer, it'll be a dry camp for us both tonight, I reckon. I'll be back by morning. If you need help, send up smoke and I'll be there." He paused, staring down. "I'll bet there's ten thousand rattlers in them rocks."

"There's three or four runnin' loose up here, too. Be ready to shoot. Those fellers are mean and they play rough."

The trail was easy to follow. Buck trotted over rolling benchlands. Tracks of six shod horses that had passed more than two weeks before were seen in grass and in sandy spots. Cameron thought three horses were being led. That meant there were three wounded or dead men along.

The bench ended in broken lava country formed by long extinct volcanic action. Scratches of the iron horseshoes showed on flat rock, but before it grew dusk Cameron headed back to the rim.

Denny looked for a way down the cliff, exploring every crevice until he found his trail, almost falling once, but saved by a single tough-rooted shrub.

At the base of the cliffs he walked through weathered rubble out onto sagebrush flats, and in fading daylight came to the white rock. He crawled over boulders splashed with buzzard dung back to the very base of the cliff. The air was foul with its odor and the putrid smell of decaying flesh. Near the broken, sl ttered wreck of the wagon was a grisly pile of rags and bones, the rotting skeleton of Max Blecker, breastbone shattered by a slug. From under the wagon, Denny pulled more rotting remains. A few hanks of blond hair hung from the skull shattered by a bullet—all that was left of Hezikiah Blecker.

Denny found the double-barreled shotgun, fired once but not reloaded. He pulled a shovel out of the wreckage. The mare's carcass lay bunched in rocks, a bullet hole between the eyes. Two things unaccounted for—the gold the boys had carried and the army Colt that had belonged to Cap'n Blecker, probably taken by the cutthroats who had murdered the boys and stolen the gold.

Night passed. On the bench above, Cameron waited for dawn, and when it came he shouted to Denny. In the quiet, they called their news and plans back and forth. Denny would bury the boys' remains, then head west to the distant road. Cameron would return to where the hold-up had taken place after unraveling tracks and analyzing those on the rim. They no longer feared an ambush. The killers had left the country.

Buck nipped sage and bunch grass while Cameron puzzled over faint signs. He decided only two men had done the work here, the other, wounded, had lain to one side. Two men had rolled the dead pony but it hadn't quite gone down. They had sat, braced their backs, and shoved the carcass over with their feet. Boot tracks went to the wounded man and horse tracks went off in the direction he had taken the evening before. He knew now that the Blecker boys had cut down half the bunch, with only two men left in good health. In this sparsely inhabited land, loss of two men and the wounding of a third would not pass unnoticed.

The buzzards came back. As the sun climbed, the huge black birds with scrawny red necks and hooked beaks flapped from their night perch on crags and in juniper trees to soar upward in ever-widening circles. On the bench, Cameron watched. Below, the whiskered miner looked heavenward. A buzzard passed within fifty feet of Cameron, dropped below the rim close over Denny, the wagon wreckage, and death, then swung east. Above him, a great wheel of fifty birds kept track of the scout. From the ground below, Denny saw the flock move eastward. After a long wait, he heard a shout from above. Cameron was pointing.

"They're dropping down to feed. Stay here till I come back!"

14

JOINED FORCES

CAMERON RODE ALONG the rim and bore to the
south where a few buzzards still circled. There he
dropped Buck's reins and walked to the edge.

The black scavengers perched on rocks,
crouched, pecking and clawing at something dead
there. Two birds farther away jumped up and down
as they tore strips of clothing or flesh loose. Cameron had found the dead bandits.

He could see no place to climb down. Nothing to do but ride back to where Denny was working. "Bill," he called, "I found them half a mile up. If you go that way you'll run right into 'em. I'll head back to the road, ride down below this cussed rimrock and come back to help yuh."

"I hear you. Go on. Look for water."

"I'll sure do that. So long."

Halfway to the road, he went down the little dry creek they had ascended the day before and trotted Buck under the rim to where the old man was burying the Blecker boys. The vultures flapped noisily as the men, their work finished, approached the new feeding ground. All that was left of the two bodies there was rags, bones, dried skin and hair. The gruesome skeletons lacked boots and clothing, stripped from them, perhaps, to delay identification or give the carrion birds quicker pickings.

They gathered rocks and piled them over the bones, wiped their faces and hands with their kerchiefs, and headed back to the waterhole. Water from the spring under the aspens was cool and sweet. They drank, washed up, let Buck roll in the sand, then watered and tied him. Cameron put the coffee pot over a small fire Denny had started and made a meal.

"The kids killed a couple and winged at least one more before they got it," Cameron mused. "But where'd the rest go? That's godforsaken country."

"I figger they live somewheres close to Willer Springs or Hooper's Bend. If we check on fellers that don't show up as usual we might find out somethin'. Cameron, somebody knew the boys were due to leave. They left twelve hours earlier'n they'd planned. It maybe got out next day in the Bend. Somebody coulda rode them down to locate 'em, then rounded up the gang and made the play."

Cameron sipped his coffee. Yes—someone close to the Bleckers must have known the boys were hauling high-grade ore. "Bill, I gotta ask you if your ore's worth enough so men would kill an' risk their own lives."

"There was fifty pounds in the box Loper took, better'n ten percent gold. That's five pounds of pure gold, smelter prices twelve dollars an ounce. Let's see. . . ." He was quiet a moment. "I'd say Loper's box was worth seven hundred'n fifty."

"Ever spell that out to anybody?"

"Nope. Anybody saw the box and felt the weight of it might think it was all gold and figger forty-fifty pounds. At a hundred and forty-four bucks a pound they'd risk it. Lope only worked for me a week before we packed the ore down and weighed it at Jervis's store. Somebody mighta thought, after Max worked for five or six weeks, then come out, got the pony shod and the wagon fixed, that he was 'bout to haul five er six times as much."

Cameron smoked. To outlaws not familiar with mining and smelting processes, values of gold ore and pure gold, it might be logical to think Denny's boxes held pure gold. He made some mental calculations. "So between the two boxes yuh actually lost about four thousand instead of the thirty they mighta figgered they got?''

''I believe they figgered it was the pure quill. And they'd never have jumped the stage and shot Loper if they was old-timers at the gold game. Their problems are jest beginnin'.''

''Yer way out in front of me.''

''First it has to be assayed. The feller at the assay office always asks where it come from, and mister, you better have an answer ready. No more secret stuff—the miners seen to that. You tell him the name of the claim, where it is, who owns it, and if it's registered. If they told the assay man it come from someplace a couple-three hundred miles away, that'd be the second big mistake. The man'd know they was lyin'. So he figgers they stole it. Gold from one place has characteristics like gold from no other place, its fineness, color, and other things a good assayer kin spot.''

It was hot even in the shade. Buck stood near the aspens, flipping his tail at troublesome flies. Cameron thought about the Bleckers and the outlaws, dead under that rock rim. He gazed through glimmering heat toward the lava country. Who in Hooper's Bend had acted as tip-off? ''Bill, how long're we gonna keep after this business of trailin' 'em down?''

''I ain't quittin' till the sons-a-bitches're all dead.''

Cameron spoke low. ''Reckon my answer's the same. If there's fellers loose in those hills who'll murder kids for a bunch of rocks they're jest guessin' at, they'll sure as hell kill anybody with something of value they can see. We got cattle."

"I'm sure glad yuh showed up, Cameron. I'll maybe hitch a ride on the stage, make the rounds of the assay offices, do some checkin'. You could talk to the doc treated the gunshot wound, and check on fellers who've left the country."

"Okay, you work on who's got the gold and I work on trailin' 'em down."

"Stage bound south should come along about dark," Denny said. "I'll flag it down. I figger it'd be better if nobody knows we're working together, except for the Bleckers and Levi Esch, of course."

Cameron replied. "You can get in touch with me through him. How can I reach yuh in Virginia City?"

"Jones and Jones assay office have done my work for years. Leave any message with them. Now if you go to Dayton, come around the lake and drop into their place, see what I've come up with. From then on, it's each man for himself. I'll give Jones and Jones instructions that if I get bumped off you're to administer my estate. See that the Bleckers, what's left of 'em, get half, and my heirs the other half. If yuh get killed, Levi Esch can handle it. How's that?"

"Fine. I don't figger on you or me gettin' killed, though."

Denny's face was bleak. "I had no idea of such a thing when I sent the Blecker boys with the gold."

"Say, Bill, how'd yuh ever happen to find gold up there in the craggies?"

"I come up the American River, tried the

Feather—that's a rough country. I heard about gold strikes over in the Boise Basin, headed that way, but stopped this side of the line and started panning. I found color and traced it, picked up a little float, finally found a stringer of ore and kept after it. I had high hopes for it a couple weeks ago but just before Max left with the ore we set off some shots. When we mucked out the stuff, all I could find of the vein was little stringers, none big enough to work. The Ajax ain't in any fault zone that I know of, and maybe I can pick it up a little deeper. Right now it won't pay its way."

"It's a hell of a note when a feller works years and figgers he's close to the real lode, then loses everything he was trailin'. Like losing a herd in a Texas norther, I reckon. Denny, will Cap'n Blecker ever get cured of what ails him?"

"Danged if I know."

Cameron rolled over on his back and pulled his hat over his eyes. "I'll ask that doc in Dayton about the cap'n. If you're gonna catch that stage, better get some shut-eye. We'll cache the boys' things here. When there's a chance to haul 'em home, I'll do it."

Old man Denny nodded agreement, pulled his wide-brimmed hat over his eyes, and slept in the shade.

15

THE DOCTOR AT DAYTON

"MISTER CAMERON, YOU'VF told me a tale and asked questions about who I treated, when and what for, but that doesn't mean I'll convey information to you. You'll have to have an officer of the law with you before I'll do that." The doctor spoke positively.

"Well, Doc, where you come from that's the way it works, but not out here. In this territory, gunshot wounds ain't confidential information."

"I'd go to the law. Why don't you do the same?"

"Dammit, man, I've rode over two hundred miles to ask you to help me unravel what happened up there. No law officer in this territory would do that, no more'n I could get you to go see a sick man I know of way up in my country."

"What makes you think I wouldn't go to see him?"

"Because he's never been able to get a doctor to look at him yet, and the stage passes less'n a mile away."

"Why not? Has he got leprosy?"

"Nope. Got shot up in the war, minie ball busted his head. Sometimes he's chipper as a daisy, then he falls down an' stays unconscious for a couple weeks."

"Sounds hopeless to me."

"Yeah, 'bout as hopeless as findin' the fellers murdered his three sons. But by God, I'm not givin' up. There's three motherless children left, two girls, and a small boy. Hell of a fix."

"Cameron, you've aroused my interest. These boys were murdered, you say."

"They worked for an old miner had some gold ore to ship out. The oldest boy carried it in a box on the stage. Hold-up men stopped 'em and blasted him with a sawed-off shotgun. Then his two brothers, couple months later, started for the assay office in Virginia City, more of Denny's gold ore in their wagon. They never showed up. Four, five days ago, I started searchin'. Found where the hold-up took place, and what was left of them and their wagon an' pony. I found two dead bandits, too—killed with buckshot from the kids' gun. People out west won't put up with anybody that helps thieves and murderers and keeps still about it. If yuh refuse to cooperate with me yuh'll have to quit fer lack of practice. Honest people still outnumber outlaws in this country, thank the Lord."

The two men looked at each other.

"I see what you mean, Cameron. I agree. And tell me where the man with the injured brain lives. Could he be brought here?"

"Doc, if I can run the outlaws down they'll be taken to Hooper's Bend for trial, if they're still alive. You'll have to come there as a witness. The sick man lives nearby—yuh could see him at the same time. But if you go sooner, I'll lay out half the cost now, the rest when yuh make the trip."

"That won't be necessary. You say you found two dead outlaws here in the Nevada territory?"

"Just across the line. Their friends had stripped 'em of most of their duds and the buzzards didn't leave much else."

The doctor leaned back in his chair. "The fellow who came here said they'd had a fight with claim-jumpers south of the lake. One, a young fellow with a six-pointed star tattooed on his left forearm, had a buckshot wound in that arm, not serious, and a furrowed cut along his ribs. I patched him up. The other man was older, had dark hair worn long, bad teeth, chewed tobacco. A pistol bullet had struck him on the right side of the chest, missed his lung by an inch."

"When was it they come in?"

"Late on a Monday evening, July thirteenth. I

made a note of it in my day ledger, charged them five dollars.''

''The Blecker boys was killed the night of the tenth.''

''Those fellows didn't look like highly respected citizens.''

''Give yuh any names?''

''Told me George Flevins and Pete Oslo, from the south end of the lake country. Oslo said he knew a fellow once that got shot right through what he called the wishbone. Said he lived for a time—it was too far to get him to a doctor—and wanted to know if they could have done anything to save his life.''

Cameron grimaced. ''I think that partic'lar feller's layin' back in a hideout, dead or dyin'.''

''If the bullet didn't shatter the breastbone, I'd say he might make it. There's little chance of infection in this dry desert air. If it smashed his wishbone, it would take a miracle to keep him alive.''

''Well, Doc, if you can go to see Cap'n Blecker in Hooper's Bend, I'll leave a hundred in gold in Levi Esch's office in Willow Springs for yuh.''

''I'll go first chance I get.''

''Just tell the Bleckers yuh heard about the cap'n. Don't mention me, they're kinda proud, savvy?''

''I'll respect your confidence.''

''So long, Doc. Thanks.''

From inside his office, Dr. Millard Marsh watched the cowman mount his buckskin saddlehorse and ride away. He had a liking for

Cameron. He would visit Hooper's Bend when first frosts cooled the weather.

In Carson city, Bill Denny asked at the Watson Assay Office if any of the particular kind and quality of ore he showed them had been brought in.

"Yes, Mister Denny," Jay Watson himself replied. "We had a sack of ore from that same prospect brought in for us to assay and sent to the smelter. Had to put the man off for a week or so—we were behind on our work. Here's the reports. That ore from your mine?"

"Yeah, it was stolen on its way here. Have you given the feller any money?"

"No, he was a new miner. We expect him here to collect any time."

"What name'd he give you? Where'd he say his prospect was?"

"Barney Welch. Said his prospect, The Lucky Stiff, was east of Honey Lake in unsurveyed territory."

"Never heard of the feller, never heard of the mine. That ore was stolen from persons in my employ three weeks ago, July tenth, to be exact. Watson, I'm placing a legal claim on that gold and the assay reports. You notify the law when Welch comes to pick up the money. How many pounds of ore did he leave?"

"An even forty. Ran eleven percent good quality gold. How's the vein running?"

"Pinching out on me. Jay, I'm going on to check other offices. This is only about a fifth of what was stole from the Ajax. It was all like this, handpicked. I'm headin' for Jones Brothers in Virginia

City now and I'll see yuh in a day or so. Watch out for that Welch. He's fast with a gun.''

At the Jones' assay office, Denny outlined briefly what had happened to his ore and to the Blecker boys. Jones had received none of the ore so far.

Denny drew a few hundred dollars from his account and went back to Carson City. Welch had not shown up yet. The old miner informed the town marshal of the robbery and the deposit of gold at the Watson office, then rented a room across the street from Watson's from which he could watch the entrance.

Cameron found Denny in Carson. Now they knew the Bleckers had seriously winged the hold-up men. Cameron would head north and start looking for cripples and the gang's hideout.

Levi Esch had been listening for rumors. He heard that Denny had flagged the stage and ridden into Carson City alone, but no one that came through told him anything about Cameron and his buckskin horse. He heard a story that the Blecker boys had lit out for Sacramento with the gold and would never chance a return to Hooper's Bend. More news going around was that a rancher named Ed Logan had been trying to break an outlaw horse when it reared backward and crushed his chest. Ed had never seen a doc in his life and had no intention of seeing one now. He was in bad shape.

Jack Logan, Ed's brother, came to Willow Springs for supplies and whiskey. Usually he made his purchases in Hooper's Bend. Eppling, the owner of the saloon, had asked him how things were going and he'd replied that he'd had to can a couple of buckeroos. They spent too much time off the job. Last he knew, they were headed for Texas.

Late one evening a tall man on a travel-worn buckskin came to Willow Springs and stopped at Levi's place. He had his pony put in Esch's stable, and rented a room for the night. Here, in Esch's Boardinghouse & Hotel, Cameron bathed and shaved. Resting, he heard Esch's soft knock. "Come on in."

Esch took a quick look around. "Best to talk before something comes up to distrurb us," he said. "What do you know now?" He went to look out the window, down the dusty street and across to Eppling's saloon.

"Mr. Esch, if you'll give me any rumors you've picked up through the grapevine, I'll try to match 'em with what me and old man Denny've turned up."

Levi found a straightbacked wooden chair, carried it to a corner away from the door, and sat down. "Mr. Cameron, there's things I've speculated about. First, there's a story the Bleckers ran off with the gold, took a cut-off to the Walker City road to Sacramento or San Francisco and won't never return them. Ed Logan, a scab-rock cattleman and horse-trader hereabouts, got crushed by a horse that r'ared back on him. His brother Jack let it out he'd fired two riders from their ranch. They took off in the general direction of Texas."

"Denny and I did some tall trailin'," Cameron said. "On the night of July tenth, near as we could find out, the Blecker boys got held up by six horsemen. The kids fired at 'em and killed two men. Those might be the ones went to Texas. They wounded another guy, least he bled like a stuck hog and had to be carried. Maybe he's the one the horse tromped on at the ranch. But they'd killed the Bleckers, both shot in the head, afterward to make sure. The outlaws put the dead and wounded in the Bleckers' wagon, headed out across lava and grass four, five miles, and come to rimrock. They laid the bleedin' feller out while two of 'em unhitched the pony, slung the Blecker boys over the rim, then shot the pony and rolled her and the rig over. They headed east another mile, stripped the two dead fellers, and heaved 'em over for the buzzards and coyotes, then went on with the wounded man and their ponies. Me an' Denny didn't follow that trail. Denny buried the Bleckers and me and him piled rocks on the outlaws' remains.'' Cameron sighed. ''We carried the boys' shotgun and some other things back to where we'd camped near the pass. Denny caught the stage that night for Carson City and I followed on my pony and went to Dayton to see a doctor name of Millard Marsh. He finally told me he'd treated a couple men for buckshot wounds, one young one named George Flevins, light hair, had a six-pointed star tattoo on his left forearm. The other called hisself Pete Oslo. He talked about a feller he knew got hit in the wishbone. Coulda been the feller the horse r'ared back on. Denny found out a man named Welch tried to get money for forty pounds of gold ore at Watson's Assay Carson City. That office and Jones and Jones at Virginia City're waitin' for him to show up. Both of 'em know Welch's ore come from Denny's mine."

"Cameron, we'll need to make certain we have the right man. If we move in on the Logans and make one mistake we'll flush the rest of the birds without getting a shot. Who in hell tipped them off about gold ore leaving town?"

Cameron smiled. "An old-timer like you'd be better at answerin' that."

"Mr. Denny suspect anyone?"

"He thought it might be good to check up on people around Hooper's Bend. I'll talk to the Blecker girls."

"Give 'em my sympathy. See you next trip."

"So long, Mister Esch—good luck."

It was hot in Cameron's room. Rowdy miners and cowboys laughed and raised hell in Eppling's saloon. It was after ten-thirty before he got to sleep.

After Cameron had ridden away to catch up with Denny, loneliness and hopelessness almost got the best of Millie. Hard work kept her from giving way to the spectre of being without help should anything happen to the two men on her brothers' trail. The cow and her calf, the chickens, pig, and Rascal the pup thrived. In the garden, beans, corn, tomatoes and melons flourished. Had they lost the boys for some reason or plan the Lord had that she could not see?

She got up at dawn, amazed to find her father trying to walk outside. She helped him into his chair and asked him what he wanted for breakfast.

"First, tell me what day it is and how everything's going." His words came slowly.

"It's almost first of August. Everything's fine, Paw. Garden's full o' vegetables, we got a cow and chickens. There's a pig in the pen and a pup fer the kids. Could you be eatin' eggs and cornmeal cakes? There's coffee, too—a real breakfast."

"I'm hungry, clear-headed, and happy to see you around. Max still at the mine?"

"I reckon Lou an' Manny're asleep. Max . . . him an' Kiah left fer Virginia City with a load of Mister Denny's high grade. They hain't come back yet."

He tipped his head back. "Well, I'll set here and think, soak up this mornin' air."

Millie got breakfast. She hated to have her father worry while he was conscious. If he didn't sink back into a spell before long, maybe there'd be a way to tell him. At breakfast, they talked of the trade with the Klingers, and the coming of Cameron, who had made it all possible. Amos Blecker asked who the cowboy worked for, then about Mr. Denny's gold mine and how long Max would work at the Ajax.

Millie broke down. "Paw, I cain't say . . . Max an' Kiah been gone more'n two weeks an' hain't been seen ner heard of. Mister Denny come down here and went south lookin' fer 'em. Mister Cameron came along an' follered him. They ain't come back ner sent word. There ain't but three of us kids left t' watch out fer yuh now."

Amos Blecker cursed his helplessness. "Has Mister Jervis stood by?"

"Yeah, he's been good. I trade eggs an' butter at

his store an' Manny sweeps out fer him. I work in town. I saved up a little money Max earned."

"Did you ask Jervis about homesteadin'?"

"Paw, he did say he'd try t' locate a place fer us. But I want t' talk t' Mister Cameron 'bout it, too."

"Does Mister Cameron interest you as a possible husband, Millie?" Her father's soft-spoken question came abruptly, and he saw her blush.

"I . . . ain't thought o' that, Paw. I only seen him a few times. I . . . trust him, though."

Amos Blecker was awake and clear-headed until evening. Then he slipped back into unconsciousness. Millie was head of the family once more.

16

FLORA MILLER'S BUSINESS AT HOOPER'S BEND

FLORA MILLER WONDERED when the BMT Cattle
Company ramrod and his men would come back.
Cameron interested her. He seemed different than
most cowboys, a good spender if turned loose. His
money was what Flora wanted.

August was a slack month. In the heat and dust,
when men did come to town they were thirsty, and
stopped first in the saloon. By the time they made
it up her stairs, in their drunken condition they

spent little time or money on the girls. Flora Miller kept records. Nowadays it wasn't like it used to be—miners scattered all through the hills, every stage loaded with men. Still, business was good enough to stay put and take in what trade came along.

By the middle of September, when first frosts colored cottonwoods along the river and choke-cherries in the lava gulches, when cattle put on the last of their fat from the drying grasses, her trade would pick up. After the winter passed, June would be the best month of the year—men, parties, and money. More travelers with hard cash came in, for June did something to men that made them ride long distances for sex and excitement at her place. On the warm June nights it really cost money to hire the whole house or the big room with the mirrors.

Flora went to San Francisco. There she investigated something new. Chinese slave girls could be bought on the wharves there. Flora saw possibilities for them in her place at Hooper's Bend. When the gold rush came, many Chinese had been imported for labor and menial services, but only men at first. Then shiploads of Chinese women were contracted for in Chinese ports, shipped to the American West, sold at auction, and taken into brothels. Flora Miller decided to try one or two. The curious would come to see if the stories they'd heard about Oriental women were true, and Flora would have cheap servant help she could use in slack times.

But she also needed a girl with beautiful, natural

red hair. Alice was leaving. She sized up the women and girls in Hooper's Bend. She knew some of their husbands, sons, and brothers far better than they did. Many house girls had come from small towns, having been introduced to sex and then trapped by circumstances. A girl in trouble was easy to persuade, Flora mused. Millie Blecker . . . if she could get that girl. . . . Her old man couldn't do much to protect her. Her brothers—hell, they wouldn't be around to object and people in the town would take little notice of her disappearance. She might get Millie to do odd jobs here, than approach her, or see that some smooth-talker got her into the bushes and in trouble. No hurry, she'd think of something.

At last a Methodist preacher came to Hooper's Bend. Douglas MacClure was young, married, and had two children. He needed a church building. People interested expected him to use the schoolhouse until land and materials could be found for a house of worship. Young, strong, and ambitious, MacClure had grown up in the wild western country. After he studied to become a preacher, he based his life work on what he perceived rather than following dogma and doctrine. He knew that he couldn't overcome sin and change sinners alone, but he would get all the help he could from the Lord and the community.

Mrs. Warren and other women persuaded their husbands to buy a house for the preacher located two blocks behind the general store on Main Street, near a vacant lot on which a church might be built. The Warrens, the Blakeleys and the Laytons lived close to the "parsonage." Ben Jervis didn't take much interest in the church. His wife and the other women met, prayed, and discussed the Bible. Jervis's wife tried hard to convince him he should lend his support. When the preacher entered the store one morning Jervis was sure he wanted a contribution of money or materials for the church.

"Good morning, Mister Jervis."

"Mornin', parson. We're cleaning' up a bit. Parson, you met Miss Millie Blecker"

"Pleased to make your acquaintance, Miss Blecker."

When Millie felt his strong clasp, she looked up into MacClure's wide-set gray eyes. The smile on his face gave an impression of frankness and honesty.

"Pleased t' meet yuh, Mister MacClure. We been wonderin' when a preacher'd come t' town."

"Have you now? That's interesting. How far away does your family live, Miss Blecker?"

"We live down the river jest above the lower crossin'. I hain't got no mother—died years ago. My paw's at home an' a sister an' brother. The other two boys is away."

"I'd like to call on you sometime, Miss Blecker."

Suddenly Millie was self-conscious and awkward. "I cain't say the day jest now. I work, and I cain't plan far ahead."

"Maybe you could stop in at the house and meet my wife. You and your family will be welcome in our new church."

As the two talked, Jervis realized he would not get off without a contribution. Would it be money, lumber, or food? He'd have to set an example—it would be free advertising, might even help some things he did get overlooked. He broke in. "Mister MacClure, what can we buy the lot for right now? Better make a deal before the price goes up."

"We can get it for twenty-seven dollars," MacClure replied. "Once the contract's signed, I intend to start the foundation and do most of the work myself."

"Well, I'll start the ball rollin'," Jervis told him. "Here's five dollars. When you need nails and lumber, come around. Reckon I could give you ten percent off all you buy for your family at the store, too."

"Why, that's wonderful, Mister Jervis. We need more people like you."

"Best thing to do is go around and see everybody. What'll the Ladies' Circle do?"

"They'll have socials and contribute what they make. It's up to me to raise all I can quickly as possible so I can start building this fall. Thank you, Mister Jervis, I'll be on my way. God bless you and your wife."

MacClure walked out the door, and a few minutes later Jervis's next caller came in at the back, almost furtively.

"Mornin', Mister Jervis. I'm out of a few things. That box of tonic I ordered come in?"

"Yeah. How many bottles yuh want? They come twelve to a box."

"I'll take a whole box." Flora lowered her voice. "Ben, is that the oldest Blecker girl?"

"Yeah," Jervis whispered.

"I don't suppose you could persuade her to come and see me. There's sewing work she could take home to do. I guess she could use the money."

They moved farther away from where Millie worked. "Well, if there was a favor or two for me in it . . . ."

"I understand. You'll ask her?"

"Let me handle her. What else do yuh need?"

On the other side of the store, the girl with the glowing red hair went on dusting and cleaning.

17

THE PARSON AND HIS FLOCK

IN HOOPER'S BEND, opinion was divided on the establishment of a preacher and his church. The saloons and Flora's House of the Red Curtains thought it would curtail their business, but other merchants felt their trade might profit thereby. Folk in town and surrounding countryside welcomed MacClure's coming, believing the church would draw law-abiding people together in a common bond. One family, the Warrens, had children and knew well the rougher elements' influence. Frank Warren had made his stake in the gold country above Marysville, then sent east for his family, picking as home the town of Hooper's Bend because it was high and dry and the climate might help his wife's lungs. She had wanted a church in the community, and it was Frank Warren who had kept after the Methodist Board to send a young, vigorous preacher to establish a church in Hooper's Bend. Mrs. Warren was kindly and tried to think the best of everyone. There was little she condemned but she felt only pity for the girls in the House of the Red Curtains. And she regretted that the grown men who ran the saloons could stoop so low as to sell their fellows the cursed drink.

Mrs. Warren had found work for Millie Blecker and when family clothes grew too small, Mrs. Warren had passed them on to her. She had encouraged Millie to better herself. Millie could learn sewing, she said, and she paid Agnes Millsap so that Agnes could pay Millie something. Together the two made dresses for Mrs. Warren and her daughter. When the MacClures had come, Mrs. Warren saw to it they were made welcome in the town. Frank Warren had stayed in the background, a big, stooped man with powerful hands and arms, his slate-gray eyes keen and inquiring. Just to look at him impressed most men. The Warrens were financially independent. They had a good library and were proud of it. They liked to read and talk, and could always be counted on to attend school gatherings.

Rousty Collins's bartender looked up to see the

new preacher entering the swinging doors of the Bar Nothing Saloon.

"Good morning, I'm Douglas MacClure, the new preacher. "You Mister Collins?"

"Mornin' Mister MacClure. Mister Collins ain't in yet. Fellers around here call me Jake, but I useta be Ralph Potter."

"I'll call you Mister Potter, if you don't mind. You work for Mister Collins and it's your way of life. I work for the Lord Jesus and it's my way of life. I came around to get acquainted. If Mister Collins comes in, tell him I called."

"If yuh don't mind a stupid question, Mister Mac, kin anybody give t' yer church?"

"The church belongs to everyone. I'm here to help it grow."

"How about buryin' fellers? You turn down people like them who lives upstairs?"

"They're the Lord's own people. I'm just here to do His will. If they die, I'll bury them and if they're ill I can try to help heal them. If they come to me to be married, I marry them."

"Mister Mac, I might need yuh t' say a few words fer me someday. Here's a ten-spot fer the church. Don't mention my name."

MacClure smiled warmly and turned to go. "Mister Potter, you have your conscience. I'm at your service."

By noon, MacClure had a hundred dollars in cash and more promised; he silently thanked the Lord for His generosity. After the midday meal, he paid for the lot. The Methodist Church of Hooper's Bend had a place on which to build its house of worship. That afternoon he borrowed a wheelbarrow, filled holes, picked up stones and refuse. As he worked on the new lot he dreamed of the building he wanted. By suppertime, his hands were sore, his face sunburned.

In the saloon, Rousty Collins heard the faint clang of iron from the smithy, an occasional tap of heels on the floor above. Jake took him a beer. "Well, Jake, what's new?"

"The new preacher come in this mornin' lookin' fer yuh. Jest come around t' git acquainted, he said."

"Ask for a contribution?"

"Hell, no. Surprised me. Said he was gonna build a church an' if he could be of any help, jest give a whistle. Said he'd be around again t' meet yuh. Name's MacClure. Big feller."

"What in hell? He know there's a buncha girls upstairs?"

"Said it was his job to help 'em. Sure wasn't holier-than-thou about it," Jake chuckled.

"Jake, I've seen a lot of these song-singers and do-gooders. They'll raise hell with yuh sooner or later." Rousty Collins thought preachers were something to be tolerated, scorned and laughed at. It would take more than a preacher to run him and the girls upstairs out of town.

After Jervis finished with Flora, it was time for Millie to go home. Jervis suggested she come back in two days to help again. He knew Flora wasn't handing out charity when she had offered work for Millie, but it wouldn't hurt to suggest it to the girl—maybe he could profit by it, too.

Millie had earned twenty-five cents. Mr. Jervis had been kind. She liked the new parson, his strong hand-clasp and kind face. She wondered about his wife and children, how he would build a church. Cameron came to her mind. Lou was certain Mister Cameron would find the boys and bring them back. Lou had more faith in Cameron than any other person in the world. He seemed to give her a long-denied sense of security. But Millie felt differently. She liked him, thought him smart, hard-working and honest. But why did he want to help them? Supposing to be tending a ranch almost a hundred miles to the north, he'd gone out of his way to come when they'd asked. And what had he gotten out of a trade that brought new ease to the Bleckers' life?

The night Millie dreamed a tall, strong man came up behind her and clasped her in his arms, caressing her until she began to respond. Just as she turned to meet his lips and see his face, she awoke, her rough flour-sacking pillow pressed against her face, her body moving against a ridge in the corn-shuck mattress.

When Millie came home the next day after working for Mrs. Engstrom, she found more trouble. Manny had a black eye and scratched face, one hand swollen and bandaged. Lou had milked the cow and done most of the chores.

"Who'd yuh fight, Manny?" Millie asked.

"Charlie Mitchell. I had a right, too. Didn't I, Lou?"

"Reckon yuh did."

"I met Charlie an' some kids back o' Jervis's

store. He asked me where was Max and Kiah an' I said I didn't know. They all haw-hawed an' started singin', 'Max is a rascal, Kiah is a thief, Max stole the gold, Kiah stole the beef.' I got Charlie down an' made him tell what he was talkin' 'bout. He heerd his dad tell his mother that people in the saloon said Max and Kiah had stole Mister Denny's gold an' gone clean t' Sacramento. Weren't never comin' back.''

"You tellin' the truth, Manny?"

"Cross my heart an' hope t' die. Jack Robbins said he heerd it too. Said his folks didn't believe it.''

"Somebody started that story fer a reason. If we jest go on doin' what we're s'posed t' be doin' maybe it'll die. The truth'll come out," Millie said stoutly.

"Millie, do yuh think they'll ever come back?" Manny's bruised lip quivered.

"Wisht I knew, Manny. I know they did right, whatever happened. They're honest an' true—you know that. Mister Denny an' Mister Cameron're lookin' fer 'em. They'll tell the town the boys didn't steal the gold. People better listen to 'em.''

18

CAMERON RETURNS

CAMERON LOPED INTO Hooper's Bend early in the morning. He felt impelled to go to the Bleckers at once, somehow give them the terrible news he had, and hear what they had to tell him.

Millie was up. At Rascal's bark she stepped out, heard Lou say, "Keep still, Rascal! That's Mister Cameron. He's our friend."

Millie saw Buck's ears point ahead to where Lou held the black pup, pink tongue lolling ahead with excitement. Cameron lifted his hand. Millie looked at him, pleasure warming her.

149

"Lou, I see Rascal's got more on his mind than chasin' squirrels. Mornin', Miss Millie, I'm in time for breakfast again."

"Good mornin', Mister Cameron. I kin fix somethin' in a minute. Lou, take Mister Cameron's horse. She kin handle him, cain't she?"

"Sure. I'll take off the rigging. Lou can take him down to the sand and let him roll. Say, your tomatoes have come on like crazy. Everything looks good."

"Wash up—I'll go in an' put on the coffee. I expect yuh found out somethin'. You kin tell me while I git things t'gether."

Millie disappeared. Cameron washed, and dried on a clean towel hung beside the outdoor basin. Millie was busy around the fireplace when he went in, found a stool, and seated himself.

"Millie," he began, "how's your Paw? Did he come to while I was gone?"

"Monday he was fine all day." She turned to face him. "How do yuh like yer eggs?"

"Over easy. Coffee sure smells good. That bacon you're fryin'?"

"Yeah. Makes eggs taste better. Kin yuh eat four?"

"Three's better."

"I'll cook four an' eat one with yuh." There was comfort in his presence as she prepared food and served him. As they sat down, she asked. "Did yuh catch up with Mister Denny?"

"Yeah. Third day out, in a dry wash east into the territory. He's in Carson City now."

Millie turned and looked straight into Cameron's

eyes. There was fear in her own. In a low, carefully controlled voice she said, "The boys're dead . . . I know it. You an' Mister Denny buried 'em. How'd yuh find 'em?"

"Listen, girl, you've had it hard, and it ain't over with yet. You're right about Max and Kiah. Outlaw robbers again—surrounded 'em on the road in the night. One thing, though—reckon we better keep it quiet for a spell—the boys killed two of 'em and maybe fixed another so he'll never be the same. They winged two more—that's five of the bunch they left their mark on. Mister Denny and I found the two dead outlaws. We piled rocks on what was left of them . . . and we buried the boys. Some day I'll take you there . . . but not now."

"Mister Cameron, thank yuh. I don't know what we'd o' done without yuh." Her voice was dull, and she fell silent.

Cameron ate his three eggs, then spoke again. "Millie, Denny and I have a good idea what happened there in the hills after the shooting. The outlaws got the gold, killed the pony, and shoved the wagon over a cliff. We're gonna trail down the ones left—get every one of 'em."

It was quiet and cool in the room; a faint smell of smoke from the fireplace mingled with the fragrance of bacon and coffee.

"Will Mister Denny get back his gold?" Millie asked.

"He ain't worryin' about that. He's more sorry about the trouble it's brought you. He'll make it up to you some way. Millie, you got any notion who told the outlaws 'bout the boys haulin' gold?"

"Mister Cameron, right now there ain't anyone I kin think of. The boys made the plans—Max come home in the night with the last o' the ore. No one but us knew about it."

"The outlaws don't live here in town. Somebody had to ride out and tell 'em what to look for and where to stop the boys."

"Manny got inta a fight with Charlie Mitchell yesterday," Millie said. "Charlie and some other boy heerd say Max an' Kiah stole the gold, went to Sacramento, and ain't comin' back. Would a story like that start here in town, when it wasn't till I went t' the sheriff that anyone knew 'bout gold ore in the wagon?"

"It's gotta tie together some way. Did yer paw ask about Max an' Kiah?"

"Yes. I had t' tell him they'd gone and hain't been heerd from."

Cameron tried to smile at her. "Millie, I reckon you're the bravest girl ever I knew. How'd he take it?"

"Like he always does—there's nothin' he can do. It's the same with me—things happen an' seems t' me like I'm standin' way off, jest lookin' on, helpless an' weak."

"Yeah. One time in a big blizzard cattle got to driftin', me and a couple other riders along with 'em. After a while it was like you said, I was outside of things, jest watchin' myself an' the critters. Time went on, cattle went down like in a dream till we came onto a ranch jest by sheer luck."

"Do yuh believe in God?"

Cameron set down his cup, reached for the makings and rolled a cigarette, lines deepening in his face, his eyes blue and intense. "Yes, I reckon I do. He looks out for people like us, not in the way of money, but showin' us how to do better, make it easier for somebody else."

"I met the new preacher tother day," Millie told him. "Name's Douglas MacClure. He wants t' come over an' visit us next week. When he opens church, we'll go. Paw wants us to."

"It would give you something to tie to in times like this."

"Will yuh go when yuh kin?"

"Sure, I will. If it's good for you, it sure cain't hurt me."

"I'd like t' have Mister MacClure say a prayer over the boys' graves. It's awful, their bein' out there alone."

"My folks're buried far from here and from people they knew. All across this country are graves. What do you think of Mister MacClure?"

"He seems like a person yuh kin talk to. He's married—has two younguns."

"I'll look him up when I'm in town today. Maybe have a talk with him. We better go out and talk with Lou and Manny."

"Iffen yuh don't mind, I wisht you'd tell 'em about the boys. It'll come better from you."

"I'll tell 'em, Millie, jest let me work up to it."

Cameron spent an hour at the Bleckers', admiring the garden and stock before he told Lou and Manny about burying their two brothers, saying that someday he would show them the graves and help put up a marker. Somehow they took it without crying. It wasn't until after he was gone that they broke down. As much a Millie wanted to comfort them, she let them alone until they relaxed.

In town, Cameron decided to talk with Sheriff Dyer. Dyer was the law in this county and must be told of the Blecker boys' death.

"Hell, Cameron, I coulda told yuh them kids was dead," was Dyer's reaction. "Their brother got shot fer pullin' a foolish stunt—it's no surprise they got plugged. You and Denny found the bodies?"

"Yeah. We buried what was left of 'em in the desert. Found where the pony was killed, too, and pushed over the rimrock."

"Any idee who ambushed 'em? How many?"

"Probably more'n three. Rain had washed out most signs. Buzzards led us to the boys' bodies. Both shot through the head."

"Anybody else know about this?"

"Not many. The sheriff at Carson City—the boys were killed in his territory. I told Millie Blecker this mornin'. Dyer, I wanta help you round up those outlaws."

"Great balls o' fire, Cameron, with nothin' to go on? Hell, the crime wasn't committed in our territory. I cain't go runnin' over there with my tongue hangin' out, bellerin' bloody murder, without havin' Dick Gray from Carson in on it. An' what kin I do here?"

"Damned if I know, Sheriff. I thought you could answer that. I jest work cattle for BMT. I never hired out to run down outlaws, but I thought when a man pinned on a shiny star, it was his job to dig into robberies and murder!''

At the mention of BMT, the cocky sheriff began to figure out where he stood. If Cameron was ramrod for BMT, a big company moving into his county, he had more behind him than the average cowpoke. If he wanted to cause trouble for the sheriff's office, he was in position to do it.

"Cameron, it's not easy t' run down hold-up men and killers. Fer one thing, nobody'll talk. 'Fraid to, I reckon. An' whenever I start a job, somebody allus tips off the fellers I'm tryin' t' ketch. Savvy?''

"I savvy, Dyer. Ever try moseying around by your lonesome? Ever ride around this country running down rumors, asking where people was at certain times? I reckon you know murderers and outlaws sometimes get caught and punished.''

"Who the hell do yuh think yuh are, anyway, trying t' tell me I ain't doin' my job?''

"Read it your own way, Dyer. Other people'll be tellin' you the same thing before long. There's a damn sight more to this business, and if one or two more get robbed and shot in cold blood folks'll squall and beller like range bulls at a waterhole. I already heard you was blind in one eye and can't see outa the other.''

The sheriff batted his eyes like a toad in a hailstorm, mouth slack in astonishment. This rider from the BMT said things he'd never thought to hear in this town. His rage got the better of his judgment.

"Git out afore I throw yuh in the jug! You may be

big stuff in Wells Crick, but by God not in this town. Yuh kin handle cows, but if yuh git t' crowdin' some fellers around here that I know of, yuh'll wake up with a spade pattin' yer whiskers, a long time dead.''

Cameron eased out of his chair, stretched, and walked to the door. "When you run for election again, Dyer, get your shoes off and plan to run right outa town. Even your tattooed friend can't save your hide. So long."

The sheriff slumped back. He had talked too much. Cameron's mention of a "tattooed friend" meant he knew about Welch. If he knew Kit Welch was in it, he must know more. Did he know who'd been killed? Had he trailed the riders beyond where the Bleckers lay? Those stupid sheep-brained idiots! They'd left marks that could be followed weeks after the job was done! There was trouble in sight.

Dyer walked to the door. Cameron had disappeared. "Prob'ly in the saloon fer a drink," he muttered. "Jake er Rousty ain't tellin' him anything, that's a cinch."

The sheriff went out the back door and over to the barn. He saddled his horse, filled a canteen at the water trough, and led the horse across the alley.

"Maw!" he called through the open door of his house. "I'm takin' a trip outa town. Put me up a little bait t' take along in my saddlebag."

Mrs. Dyer stopped dusting and went to the kitchen. She wondered where Dyer was going off to alone. Maybe it had something to do with the Blecker boy's disappearance. She didn't like the way people acted when the subject came up, almost as if they wondered if her husband wasn't trying to find them and if so, why he wasn't.

19

VIEW FROM THE ROOF OF THE BAR NOTHING

CAMERON WALKED ACROSS the street and through a narrow space between the general store and the Bar Nothing Saloon. Behind the store, his buckskin rested at the hitch rack, half asleep in the sun. The cowboy fumbled in the near saddlebag, pulled out a cloth-wrapped tube which he slipped under his vest, then turned and entered the saloon.

At the bar, Jake nodded a greeting.

"Can I get up on the roof without everybody in town knowin' where I'm at?"

"Sure, Cameron." The bartender turned and pointed to the back of the room. "Go up those stairs. At the top, 'stead o' turnin' into Flory's place, open the other door—here's the key, yuh kin leave it on yer way out. Take it easy if yuh don't wanta be seen. Flory has ears on her like a cat. Look t' the left an' yuh'll see a light from the roof. Head fer it—yuh kin raise the lid up there an' go out."

"Thanks. Don't tip anybody off."

Cameron took the key, slipped off boots and spurs, and went up with them in one hand. The door opened easily onto the gloom and musty air of an attic. He walked cautiously to the closed skylight, stepping on bits of ancient debris, walking around long-stored objects. He lifted the trap door, propped it open with a stick left there, and quickly swung up onto the roof after placing his boots before him.

The building was higher than its neighbors and he could look over roofs to the distant flatlands. He walked to the edge; he could almost have jumped across to the roof of Ben Jervis's place.

He pulled on his boots and sat in shade a few moments watching the road that ran south out of town, then clambered to where he could look out over the high false front of the saloon at the jail and the sheriff's office. A movement attracted him—a man on a horse going down the street at a trot. It was Tom Dyer, the sheriff. Cameron watched until Dyer circled out onto the main road.

Now Dyer urged his pony into a lope; dust strung out in the still hot air in a trailing ribbon.

Cameron reached under his vest. The cloth-wrapped object he had carried up from his saddle was a short brass telescope. He wiped the lens with his neckerchief, held the instrument to his right eye, and focused it. He would keep track of the man riding leisurely toward the south.

Half an hour later, the sheriff turned his pony west, the dust streak flat along the sage as the black pony loped along. Cameron's job was finished.

After the bright sunshine, he was blind in the dark, and waited for his eyes to adjust, hearing voices from some room off the hall. He couldn't make out words; two or three woman were talking.

When he could see well enough to walk without stumbling, he began to walk back to where he hoped the hall door was, each step a cautious one. Boots in his left hand, the right outthrust to feel along the wall, he found the door. When he soundlessly pushed it open, the voices were louder and he saw that the door into Flora's place was ajar. He was trapped.

All at once he heard a man's voice, one he recognized.

"You're sure yuh didn't see him come up here?"

"Yes, I'm sure. I'd like to see him come up, though, even if it is morning. Mexia'd take care of him, wouldn't you, little chili pepper? No, Ben, if he comes, I'll let you know."

"His horse's tied down below. I figgered he was in the saloon, but he ain't."

"Hooper's Bend ain't so big but what he'll show

up. Say, you had a chance to see the girl about workin' for me?''

"No, but I will. She'll be back day after tomorrow. I'll talk her into it. Don't ever let on, though. It's hard enough now to get along with my wife. So long, Flora. When your new girls come in, let me know. I'll come up early some morning and inspect 'em for yuh.''

Cameron pulled the door closed and waited for the man to leave. He heard the clip, clop of heels as Jervis went down. When the coast was clear, he stepped out to the stairs. Before he reached the bottom he pulled on his boots. At the back of the saloon Jake saw him lay down the key with a motion meaning, "Thanks!" He walked out to Buck, mounted, and trotted up the street.

Cameron suspected the man he saw working in a vacant lot was the new preacher, and pulled his pony up.

"You the new preacher?" He wanted to sound cordial; he might need this man's help.

"Yes. Douglas MacClure's the name."

"I'm Percy Cameron. I've heard about you. I'd like to get acquainted. Got time to talk?"

"Call me Mac, Cameron. What's on your mind?"

"Will anything said in confidence be treated as such?" Cameron smiled.

"Yes. I take it you want to say some things of that nature."

"I heard yuh met Millie Blecker the other day. Could you tell me in a general way what you've heard about her family. I'm a friend of theirs."

They hunkered down in the shade of a cottonwood. "I've heard the Bleckers are a proud, stuck-up family," MacClure began. "From somewhere south, they say. Some tell me Cap'n Blecker was hurt in the war, others say he's smart buy lazy. They say the kids are hard workers, but trust no one and keep to themselves. One boy was shot in a hold-up last month because he wouldn't give up some gold he was guarding. I met Millie in Jervis's store. Mrs. Warren, whom I respect highly, thinks well of her."

Cameron rolled a cigarette, scratched a match. "Well, Mister MacClure, I like the Blecker kids. Millie had a rough row to hoe. I made a deal for 'em so they could live a little better. Denny, the old miner the boys worked for, is honest and a square-shooter. When I came here I heard about the first boy bein' shot. When the next two disappeared, I come down from Duck Lake to find out what happened. My boss knows what I'm doin'. If thieves and outlaws murder kids for gold, they'll do it for cattle or money or anything else of value. I found out that the boys were both murdered and thrown over a cliff to the buzzards. Denny and I buried 'em. Mac, someday I want yuh to say a few words over their graves."

The preacher gazed at Cameron and a despairing sound came from his lips. "Gives a man a heavy heart," he said.

Cameron went on. "I saw what's left of the Blecker kids this morning. If you see Millie, talk to her. Ever been around colts?"

"Yes, I've broken a few to harness and saddle."

"Well, yuh gotta gentle Millie. She's proud and suspicious but take it easy and she'll lead right along. She needs to be told the Lord hasn't forgot her. If you can give her a feeling of confidence, the other kids'll pick it up. Right now they're ripe for any trouble."

"I understand, Cameron. I can do that."

"I'll be around in a few days. Tell the kids if they want to get word to me yuh'll see to it. They'll figger I trust yuh."

"How could I reach you?"

"Levi Esch at Willow Springs. Bill Denny's at Carson City and can be reached through the sheriff there. If anything happens to him, he says the Bleckers get half of this estate. Jones and Jones in Virginia City have the papers."

"I hope nothing happens to either of you. I'll treat what you said in confidence."

Cameron went to the buckskin, slipped his hand under the bridle headstall, and rubbed the pony's chin. "Well, I gotta be on the move. Pleased t' meet yuh, Mac. Like it here?"

"My wife can't get used to the big country, and the heat. Makes her feel like a missionary in Africa."

"Well, yuh both got missionary work cut out for yuh here. One of these days when you get the church ready and if the weather's good, figger on a BMT beef to barbecue for the crowd. Look out for the Blecker kids, and the Lord'll bless yuh for it. So long, Mac."

Cameron rode away.

From the lava ridge above the Logan Ranch,

Cameron could see all the Lazy L outfit, its buildings huddled close to the cottonwood and quaking aspen grove, a watered green strip that wound down into sage flats. Corrals of poles and sticks bound together with rawhide and wire were nearly empty. Heat waves danced and shimmered; sweat moved under his hat. There was no sign of the sheriff or his black horse in the area below, but Cameron felt sure that sooner or later the lawman would emerge from the house.

As the sun slanted toward the west, two men came out and sauntered toward the barns. Through the glass, Cameron saw the sheriff and some dark stranger stop near a shed to talk. Finally the sheriff led his horse from under the roof, tightened the cinch, and swung aboard. After further pause, he headed for the distant road home.

Cameron waited another hour before he rode into the Lazy L. No dog barked, no one called in the hot stillness. An old cat crossed from one shed to another carrying a mouse to her kittens, the only living thing that moved. The rider swung off his buckskin. A young fellow of about nineteen or twenty appeared on the porch of the house.

"Yuh lookin' fer somebody, mister?"

"Logan live here?"

"Yeah. I'm Jack Logan."

"I'm Cameron—BMT—around this neck o' the woods to get acquainted, maybe bid on any stock yuh might have to sell this fall."

"Steers? Stockers?"

"We're interested in anything that'll walk and carry its own hide." Cameron glanced about. "My gosh, it's been hot today. Always this way this time o' year?"

"Sure as hell is. Take a seat on the porch. I'll fetch a dipper o' water." Bowlegged, Jack Logan walked into the house. Cameron heard the clank of tin on a bucket, and Jack reappeared. "Jist outa the spring. Cain't be warm yet and there's no damn alkali in it." He handed the dripping dipper to Cameron. "Damned if I know what t' say about cattle. My brother Ed, he usually swings the gate in this family, got throwed a while back. Busted his wishbone. He died in a day or so. Brother Art's still away. I'm ramroddin' the outfit."

"By God, that's good water. Best drink I've had so far up here. You and your brother settle this place?"

"Yeah, we bought out a feller named Jackson several years back an' started buildin' a herd. It's good winter grass country but hot as hell this time o' the year. We heerd the BMT outfit was up at Duck Lake. Gonna locate there permanent?"

"Yeah. We got a thousand head of she-stuff up there. I rounded up sixty Durham bulls in Lost River country to put with 'em. After a few calf crops we'll move the original herd north. There's lotsa grass and we can use a couple or three thousand more now."

"We can rustle some outa the junipers an' lava if yer not partic'lar what we show up with," Logan replied. "Mebbe long about October."

"Jest so we can get 'em through the winter. You gather 'em, my boys'll work the herd. I'll pay yuh by bank draft, so much a head for cows, yearlings, steers—whatever yuh got. Wells Fargo'll honor it right in Hooper's Bend.''

"That'll be fine with me. When Art comes we'll talk it over."

"Reckon yuh could leave word with Esch in Willow Springs or Ben Jervis in the Bend when yuh're ready to deal," Cameron said.

Logan stretched his arms and relaxed. "Hell, Cameron, let's meet at the Bar Nothin' in two weeks. Flora's got a couple new girls comin' in an' I wanta be there t' see if they've got any new tricks."

"Suits me fine."

"Say, how'd yuh come t' be way out here fer cattle?"

"I aimed to cut back to Willow Springs and across to the east rim, lookin' for stock an' gettin' acquainted with the country."

"Yuh heerd any rumors 'bout them Blecker boys?"

"Hell, Logan, the Blecker kids got potted. That Sheriff Dyer's so bull-headed and stupid he won't believe it. How he ever got elected I'll never know." Cameron started for his horse. "See yuh in town."

Jack Logan rose. "Well, how come somebody just up and killed two kids on the road, Cameron?" he asked, as though he couldn't keep away from the subject.

"They was haulin' high-grade ore from old man Denny's Ajax prospect to Virginia City. Hell, if I was Denny and had that much of the stuff, I'd sell the mine and quit lookin' at the hind end of a cow."

"How much yuh figger the kids had?"

"Must've been three hundred pounds—high grade, the pure quill—worth more'n the whole herd of critters the BMT trailed in here."

"Cameron, yuh seem t' know more 'bout that there gold than the whole town o' Hooper's Bend."

"I've learned a bit here and there and I knew the kids, but my interest's in gettin' ahold of that mine or findin' the gold. If old man Denny and a kid could dig that much outa a hole in the ground in a couple months, then I'm in the wrong business."

"Hell yuh say! I allus figgered the old coot was jist playin' around up there in the Raggeds." Logan's eyes glittered.

"Some fellers never know what anything's worth and the old man might be like that. Might walk in there and make him a deal he'd take yuh up on jest so he could go lookin' for another. Why? Yuh lookin' for a mine?"

"I'm lookin' fer somethin' better'n runnin' a buncha hides and horns. With Ed gone, only reason I'm here is I ain't found it yet."

Thinking and wondering, Logan watched the buckskin singlefoot down the lane.

Cameron rode into Willow Springs at dusk and left his horse at the livery stable back of Levi's store and boarding house. Levi found a room for him. The evening meal was ready and the two men ate together, discussing casual, ordinary news. Flossie waited on them, four or five men came in to eat, then sat in the lobby and read time-tattered newspapers by the light of coal oil lamps. Moths and flying bugs skittered and fluttered around the doors; outside, day noises faded away. Cameron and Levi went upstairs. It was hot on the second floor; no breath of air moved to flutter the shabby window curtains. Dust from the road hung and lingered. Their clothes were damp with sweat.

Cameron stripped off his shirt, poured water from the pitcher on the stand into the china basin. He splashed its coolness over his neck and chest, let himself wet and, refreshed, slouched into a chair opposite the little innkeeper.

"Reckon yuh know why I dropped in, Esch. Any news?"

"Denny's still away and nobody's shown up yet. I heard Ed Logan died after the horse fell on him. His brothers buried him back of the house. Two of their men left for Texas. That's all I know. You got anything?"

"I saw Dyer, the sheriff, and put him straight on the killing, told him I thought he oughta do more work toward solving it. I mentioned something about his tattooed friend. Half an hour after that, he headed out west and south. I watched him from the roof of the Bar Nothing."

"Cameron, d' ya think that was smart?"

"Why not, Levi? They don't know all we know and they're afraid to try to find out. I rode out to the Logan spread, hid out, and saw the sheriff start back to the Bend after talkin' things over. An hour later I rode in, told Jack Logan I was after cattle. We got to chewin' the fat, and he asked me about the Blecker boys disappearin'. I told him they got killed for gold ore they was haulin'. Then he wanted to know its value and what the mine was worth. I give him a lot o' bullshit that'll stir him up.''

Levi sat and smoked, looking out the window west toward the distant lava rims, back of them the high Sierra. Flickers of lightning sparked along the sky. Somewhere a thunderstorm was brewing. ''Whaddya think of this feller Logan?''

Cameron remained silent for a time. ''I don't worry about him, Levi,'' he said at last, ''but I b'lieve him and his brothers did the job. Ed was the boss, Art's the troublemaker, Jack went along for the show. Jack can be handled when the time comes. What I wanta know is who set the Logan crowd on Denny's gold in the first place.''

In the dark, hot, unventilated room a laugh and a holler echoed from across the street as someone batted his way through the bar's swinging doors.

''Any idee other than Dyer who it might be?''

''I heard Flora Miller was bringin' in a coupla new girls. Does Flora have connections in the Bend other than Rousty Collins and the sheriff?''

''Cameron, she could have a lot of 'em. But all I hear is rumors.''

''Yuh might find out that way who the new girls are, where they're comin' from.'' Cameron paused, spoke in a different tone. ''What do yuh really know about Ben Jervis?''

Again a long silence before the old trader replied. ''I don't trust Jervis as I once did. His name keeps comin' up where it shouldn't, if yuh know what I mean.''

''Somethin' the other day made me wonder,

too, Levi. I don't intend to let Ben know I suspect him. Now I reckon I'll let my horse stay here for a coupla days while I take a run down to Carson on the stage.''

"It'll get here about six in the mornin', Rufe drivin'. I'll call yuh early—you can have breakfast with me.''

"I'll see a friend of mine there. I might get a proposition for yuh to work on. And by the way, I made a deal with the doc in Dayton to come and see Amos Blecker. Told him he could pick up a hundred in gold from you after he's made his exam. Here's a coupla slugs to give him but don't let on yuh know much. I'll see him down there. He's the one who treated them two fellers for gunshot, yuh know.''

"When can I expect to see yuh again?''

"A week. Might get in before. Keep your ears open about who's hired at the Logan Ranch. Somebody'll be getting a job over there.''

"Somebody might turn up coming through here,'' Esch responded. "I'm headed for bed. See you in the morning.''

"Good night, Levi.''

20

WHAT IS FAITH?

ATER CAMERON LEFT her, Millie faced what seemed an endless day, with others to follow. She had kept up her confidence and her faith in the future fairly well, but now she felt herself to be on a bleak, level plateau of life, time stretching before her, nothing but drudgery and loneliness ahead.

Loper was dead, buried in Willow Springs. She had never seen his grave nor talked with the man who laid him to rest. Somewhere in a sandy desert an old man and a cowboy had found Max and Hezekiah's bones where buzzards fed. Cameron had not told her how they had been killed but she knew. Each time her helpless father passed from them it was for a longer period. What would happen to her, to Lou and Manny?

Millie worked at washing clothes that day. The steaming hot water combined with desert heat became almost more than she could bear. Lye reddened her hands, bending over the wooden tubs seemed to break her back, cloying moisture curled her hair into tendrils that made her scalp itch. With relief she took down the last of the clothes from the line, folded and laid them away. She would iron in the cool of morning. On her way home, the day's heat reflected upward from the burning sand to persecute her every step.

Down near the river, Manny tended the heifer. Lou had left a note saying she'd gone to help Mrs. Smith whose sick baby had the "summer complaint." Smaller children in the town were suffering. Already two had died. In the shady spot where the river's bend made a pool under cottonwoods, Millie soon was lazing in the water. When she heard her brother call, she got out quickly and dressed, gathering her damp hair up into a knot. She couldn't quite place the man who stood with his back to her, but when he turned she saw it was the new Methodist preacher.

"Hello, Miss Blecker," he said, "I hope I'm not intruding."

"Hello, Mister MacClure. I was jist coolin' off in the river. Thought I'd melt today, washin', but I kept thinkin' of a swim and I went in soon as I come home."

The preacher smiled, then said, "We're new here and Mrs. MacClure's never lived in such a big wild country. Could you come in sometime and talk with her about how to do things and what you'd do in certain circumstances? It would make her feel more at ease."

"What kin I say to help? Mrs. Warren or any of her neighbors'd do better than me."

MacClure's smile warmed. "You're younger, close to your family, and more practical. My wife's heard of how well you manage. I'd appreciate it if you'd visit us."

"Why, 'course I will, then. Maybe I kin come after I finish ironin' tomorrow. I'll be through 'fore noon."

"Yes . . . thank you . . . come at your convenience. Say, you have a nice garden. And a cow, too—looks like a Jersey. I haven't seen one as nice since I left home in the East. Where'd you ever get her?"

Millie forgot her doubts and fears. The evening heat went unnoticed, her hair, still tied in a loose knot, no longer bothered her, and conversation flowed smoothly between them. As she gathered garden vegetables she told the preacher of Cameron's trade with Klinger, and his concern for her brothers.

MacClure replied that Cameron had come to see him and requested his presence at the desert graves when he and the remaining Bleckers placed markers there.

"Miss Millie, we can pray to God now for the boys."

"But don't yuh hafta pray in a church?"

"The Lord hears everything we say. He made the whole world and everything in it. I'll pray here and ask Him for help and to receive your brothers into the Kingdom of Heaven."

MacClure dropped to his knees in the dust. Millie knelt beside him to listen to the first prayer she had ever heard. The fact that MacClure had walked through desert sun, to pray for someone he'd never known, made an impression on her. She sensed his confidence. Her belief in life, her faith in the world in which she must live, began to be restored.

When the preacher started home, walking through the sand with a sack of garden truck slung over his shoulder, Millie began the evening meal, singing as she worked. At six o'clock the next morning she began Mrs. Blakeley's ironing, enjoying the fragrance of the hot iron on freshly washed clothing in the cool morning air. By ten o'clock she had earned twenty cents and was ready to go to the preacher's home. Mrs. MacClure asked to be called Nelly. The two talked about children and gardens and Millie told how she had come to Hooper's Bend and about people she worked for. At noon dinner she heard Mrs. MacClure ask the Lord's blessing on the food; Millie began to learn something about religion and how some people talked about God and His work. Her fears faded, new hope for the future took root in her mind, and she left promising to return soon.

The next morning was promised to Ben Jervis. Millie reached the store at seven o'clock and found the duster and dustcloth to clean off top shelves. A while later, she accidentally knocked the feather duster to the floor. She climbed down for it and heard Jervis speaking of a new job he might get for her.

"What would it be, Mister Jervis?"

"Miss Flora Miller needs a girl every mornin' to clean the rooms, sweep an' dust, even do sewin' now an' then. Oh, I know what people say about her place and the girls there but she'll pay good, a dollar a day, start at six and leave at noon, five days a week if yuh want. I told her I'd ask yuh."

Millie hesitated. She knew what the girls in the upper rooms of the Bar Nothing did for a living. Her father had warned her against women who might try to interest her and Lou into dancing with and entertaining men. Suddenly she wondered what part Jervis might have played in this proposition. "Mister Jervis, I jist took a new job an' I want t' think this one over. I kin let yuh know day after tomorrow."

"Sure, Millie." Jervis did not push. That dollar-a-day offer would win her over. "Now come out in the back room—there's some things t' be done there."

The girl followed him into the dark musty storeroom where he took tops off wooden boxes from which Millie unpacked dishes and glassware, carrying them out front. She was glad to be down from the ladder. By ten o'clock she was free to go home. Wanting someone to advise her about working for Flora Miller, she headed across to where MacClure labored, lining out the excavation for his new church. He straightened up.

"Well, Miss Millie, how goes it today?"

"Fine, Mister MacClure. Is Nelly home?"

"No, she went over to see Mrs. Dawson."

"I reckon I need advice. Mister Jervis told me 'bout a steady job I kin have . . . but I don't know."

"I'll help if I can."

"It's thisaway. He said Miss Flora Miller wants t' know if I'd work fer her in the mornings, cleanin' up, makin' beds, maybe do some sewin'. She'll pay me a dollar each mornin' I work."

"Millie, I've heard of Flora Miller. You know she employs girls who entertain men at night?"

"Yes. . . . But if I kin do the work I'll make more money. Mister Jervis seemed t' want I should take the job, but I don't think Paw would like it— Mister Cameron, neither."

"That's your answer. If you work there you'd risk your good name."

"I reckon I know what yuh mean, Mister MacClure. Should I tell Mister Cameron?"

"Someday, maybe. By the way, if you want to get in touch with him, he told me how to reach him."

Douglas MacClure decided that this approach by the woman in business above the saloon was a coolly calculated move to trap Millie, with Jervis as the go-between.

Rufe Bledsoe, riding the high seat alone, handling his four highstrung bays as easily as if they were plough horses, saw the tall cowman walk out of the hotel in Willow Springs. "Mornin', boy. Yuh kin ride up with me where it ain't so dusty, if yuh want."

"Thanks, Rufe. Should I throw my saddlebags in the boot?"

"I'll take 'em up here."

Rufe squalled at the team as they thundered out of town headed south for Virginia City. Dust rolled up behind the stage and hung in a widening cloud. Already the heat lay on desert sand, and the smell of juniper resin was strong in the tepid air.

Rufe leaned toward his companion. "Heerd yuh found extry bodies 'side the Bleckers' out there in the rimrock."

"Buzzard bait, Rufe, We piled rocks over 'em. The boys laid out three of 'em, but some're still runnin' loose."

"Best news I've heerd in quite a spell. Yuh figger the kids winged some more?"

"Outa six ridin' ponies only one got away without carrying lead or marks of it. Wanta help do a little more lookin'?"

"Long as it's on yer side, sure."

"The feller tipped off his gang to what was in that first box Loper was lookin' out for has to be the same hombre tipped 'em off when the Blecker boys headed out with another batch of ore. It don't take much thinking to realize it was somebody handy to town who knew the Bleckers. When we get that feller pegged—down comes McGinty hangin' by a rope."

"I'll sure keep my eyes peeled."

Cameron nodded approval. "I never knew

Loper," he said, "but I'm acquainted now with the rest of the family. And I know old Bill Denny. I counted myself in when this last round was dealt and I'm stickin' to see who has the joker."

Rufe chewed tobacco, finally gathering a mouthful of liquid to splash at a roadwide lava rock. This tough buckeroo might be a man to tie to, he reckoned, remembering how when little Lou Blecker sent a note, Cameron had dropped his work and headed his bronc south at a high lope to hunt down a pack of lousy coyotes.

"Wal, Cameron, it's a big rough country. Them as has, gits. Ain't no place fer psalm singers an' do-gooders. All the same, I been driving this run fer two years now an' the only trouble I ever had was the shootin' at Cow Hollow. Wouldn't o' been any then but fer than dern fool kid."

"Yes, there would, and yuh damned well know it. If he'd heaved over the box, the story would've got around and the gang would've gone ahead pickin' up whatever they could. Loper stuck with the gold. His brothers hired out to do the same thing and they went prepared. I'll bet there won't be another hold-up along this line fer some time. Two wet-eared boys with their daddy's old gun made it safe fer yuh."

"That's a hell of a thing t' say, Cameron."

"The people in this county owe a big debt to those boys but all I hear is that the kids run off with the gold." Cameron snorted in disgust.

"Wal, what yuh want me t' do?"

"Figger out who tipped off them skunks to the gold."

The heat grew stronger. Rimed with sweat, splashed with foam, the team toiled upgrade. Far to the west a flock of birds circled on wide wings the sun caught as they shifted with rising currents, tilting, following the curve. Reminded of buzzards sailing below the rim that morning to feed, Cameron ripped out an oath and kicked the apron of the stage.

"Yuh bury the boys?"

"Old man Denny had it done when I got there. All I did was smooth the graves an' listen to him pray."

"Might tell him I cut myself inta this deal clear t' the end o' the string."

"That's a help. Keep in touch with Levi Esch and MacClure the new preacher, too. If we don't clean this gang out now, we might never be able to."

At Brice's Ranch, Rufe changed teams. Three passengers got out, stretched their legs, and drank deep of cold spring water. The fresh team settled to a steady run, and in the afternoon, white-topped thunderheads rose, rolling south. Toward evening, distant thunder came to their ears. Off to the west, streaks of lightning ripped the clouds.

"We could use a little freshenin'," said Rufe.

Lightning cracked closer and a wind moved the air, with it the sweet smell of rain on dust and sage. With bright flash and tremendous crash the skies opened and rain streamed down, slanted by wind, turning to hail that rattled on team, driver, and coach. Rufe held tight to the long leather lines, feet braced for support. As the moist earth steamed, last light from the west cast an eerie golden haze. Mule deer and antelope appeared to stare at the racing stage, and birds, revived by the storm, fluttered up. A rainbow arched at the edge of the storm, reminding Rufe of the city's pleasures, the honky-tonks and bars, warm laughter and a woman's warm arms.

Rufe told of experiences on the route, of women he'd met and made love to. Cameron listened with half an ear.

"Old Flora come in several years back," Rufe was saying. "She does business all up an' down the line an' makes a trip out now an' then fer fresh fillies. Got a coupla new ones comin' in from Frisco this week. I heerd she *bought* 'em. An' she's s'posed t' be trainin' a new one she picked out from close t' the Bend."

"I don't know who that'd be, Rufe."

"Hell, I don't hafta go t' Flory's place," the stage driver went on. "Yuh'd be surprised at what all has took place in this buggy, with the high-class wimmen passengers. Once one of 'em knocked on the roof an' I hollered, 'What's wrong down there?' She says, 'Stop the stage a minnit, driver, an' help me. My sister's havin' a spell.' I pulled up, tied the ribbons, climbed down an' opened the door. I lost a half-hour that run," he crackled. laughing.

Cameron, having offered to drive, let the team travel at their own gait.

"There's somethin' funny about this Blecker bunch," Rufe resumed. "The kids've allus been suspicious of ever'body, stickin' together. The old man's looney as a hound dog with fits in July, nobody lookin' out for 'em all now 'cept you an' an old white-haired, cabin-crazy miner. Yuh don't s'pose Flory's lookin' at one of them girls t' put in her house? Millie's big enough—an' she's pertier'n a speckled pup with long ears.''

Cameron reacted carefully. "I don't know . . . how d'yuh reckon that?"

"There's others she's picked up. Like that farmer's wife out on the flats, her man allus workin', her with nothin' t' do 'cept cook, wash dishes, milk the cow, an' kill rattlers. Flory sent a feller t' make contact. She ended up in Virginia City in a crib.''

"Anybody round the Bend know about it?"

"Real nice folks suspect it, but they close their eyes. Her tryin' fer the Blecker girls makes sense. Millie's tryin' t' make ends meet and it won't work out. She might give up washin' clothes an' settle for a soft bed.''

Cameron felt a chill of alarm. Rufe could be right.

21

DENNY THINKS ABOUT RANCHING

BILL DENNY STAYED around Carson City. He spent time in the Watson assay office, visited smelters, helped grade ore, listened to mining engineers' problems, gave asked-for opinions on questions regarding various law suits of giant operators against lone miners. Now he wanted to go back to the Ajax and dig for the pinched-out vein.

The assay report and the stolen ore remained unclaimed and Denny suspectd someone had tipped off the man who had brought them to lie low and wait. Then the stage dropped Cameron in Carson City and he made his way to Denny's room.

"Cameron," the miner greeted the cowboy, "I was about to leave—go back to the Ajax. Glad you showed up. Reckon we oughta argy a bit 'bout what goes on."

"Your men ever show up?"

"Nope. Neither them nor anymore of the gold ore. What's new in the Bend?"

"I went to see the Bleckers. Cap'n's still dreamin'. All the kids doin' fine. There's a new young preacher, name of MacClure, Methodist. No psalm singer—he's already started to build a church. I sized him up, reckoned he could be trusted. I've told him about the deal to find the outlaws. He was to go see Millie, keep her steady."

"Glad yuh done that, Percy."

"He knows what your will says, all about the boys' murder, and that we're tryin' to find the tip-off man and bring 'em all to trial. One thing about a hangin'—it sure discourages fellers that see it from gettin' the same treatment."

"Yuh see Esch on your way down?"

"Yeah. Also run onto one of the fellers slung the boys over the rim."

"Who's that?"

"Jack Logan, the only one the boys didn't mark. up. His brother Ed, the one bled so bad, died a few days back. Reckon he was the one with the busted wishbone. Jack buried him there on the ranch. That leaves Art Logan and Welch—or Flevins, whatever his real name is—and the feller who tipped 'em off.

"I run into Tom Dyer, told him about findin' the kids murdered and let drop we knew a tattooed feller was in on it. Right after that, I climbed up on the Bar Nothing's roof and watched Dyer ride out. Trailed him to the Logan place. Afer he left, I rode in and chinned with Jack."

"I reckon he was surprised."

"Yeah! Ed Logan was the brains of the outfit, and Jack's lost without him. I offered to buy cattle and he went fer it. He's meetin' me in the Bend in two weeks t' clinch the deal. He mentioned the Blecker boys. I told him we found the kids murdered, that I figgered the stolen gold you and Max dug outa your mine was worth twenty-five, thirty thousand. Said you was wantin' to sell the mine and prospect somewheres else. He licked his lips at the idee."

"Sell my mine. . . ? Well, the vein's pinchin' out. I found it by followin' color in the crick to the outcrop in granite rock. The last shot opened a wall of porphyry an' the gold vein lessened. Way it stacks up now, the mine's worth whatever I kin get fer it."

"Would yuh trade it fer a ranch an' a thousand head of cattle?"

"Boy, you feelin' all right? Who'd be durn fool enough t' make a deal like that?"

"Jack Logan. Would you give me a half interest in his Lazy L to help yuh run it?"

"Percy, you serious?"

"Damn serious. Flora Miller's got her eye on the Blecker girls. I'd shoot her like the bitch she is before I'd see Millie and Lou get pulled inta her place. I'd like to settle the three Bleckers on Logan's ranch away from Hooper's Bend, able to make an honest living."

The old man nodded. He thought a girl like Millie could bring Flora and her fancy house more money than the girl could ever earn by hard work. "Percy, I trust your judgment. The mine ain't worth a plugged nickel to me as it is."

"I let Jack think all he had to do was count wheelbarrow loads an' pick out gold. We may need Esch's help. He could drop the hint you're ready to pull outa the Ajax, too. If Jack could get the mine, he could hold the gold ore the bunch stole and collect on it anytime."

"I'll be a son-of-a-goat! Percy, we'd be in the cow business for sure. Is the Logan outfit worth anything?"

"Sure is! Reckon they ain't been too interested in whose calves they brand, though. It'd be a nice place to fix up, run cows and calves on. Only seven or eight miles from Willow Springs."

"Look, boy, I got enough money laid by so I ain't hurtin'. We'll get our own back and teach those Logans how to suck eggs, too."

As much as Denny wanted to leave town, it was decided he would stay where he was a while. If Jack Logan went up to the mine on his own to inspect it, he might be ready to listen to their deal when Denny returned. Cameron took the stage back to Willow Springs. Levi Esch agreed the cowboy's plan might work. "How soon can Denny make the deal?" he asked at once.

"Anytime, Levi. Just let it drop that Denny's sick of the mine after losin' gold to a bunch of cutthroat outlaws and wants to sell or trade it off. Jack Logan's been under his brother's wing so long he don't know nothin', but he's greedy. The ranch don't mean a thing to him and he'd jump at the mine if he was egged on."

Levi grinned. "Percy," he asked, "are we any closer to knowing who tipped the Logan gang off?"

"Nope. But that'll come out. Keep your eyes and ears open on when Flora's bringin' in the new girls."

Cameron's buckskin, snorty from his long rest, pranced out as though walking on eggs; only steady hand and leg pressure kept him from breaking. Once out of town, Cameron gave him rein and the gelding plunged into a run, powerful muscles tight enough to start pitching. Cameron thought it was good to be back in the saddle and on his way to see Millie. How womanly and sweet she had become, he mused. To think of her being in a fancy house at the service of any man with money outraged him. He thought seriously about Millie's part in his life. Cameron had never considered marrying up to now, but he was deeply involved with this family, interest in them grown from casual curiosity and a desire to help, and he looked on Millie as someone he could trust and love.

Lou ran out from willow shade back of the

Blecker place when Cameron rode up. "Oh, Mister Cameron, I'm sure glad you come. Millie's in town. Kin I lead Buck down in the shade? He's all hot and sweaty—jist wait, I'll git some corn fer yuh, Buck."

Cameron took a couple of packages from his saddlebags and handed one to Lou. "Mister Denny sent yuh this," he told her.

When she opened the box, Lou gasped. A bright green ribbon, a blue one, too. A small mirror and a comb. A tear poised itself on the rosy round of each cheek and she wiped them away with her arm but their stain remained below her eyes. "Mister Cameron, that's the nicest present I ever did git."

She told him how Jervis had tried to make up to Millie and get her to work mornings for Flora Miller. "Mister MacClure told her if she thought yuh wouldn't like it, not to," she said.

Cameron had always been able to mask his emotions, but now his heart pounded and all he wanted was to smash Jervis's sneaky face again and again.

Lou went on. "Mister MacClure helped us. Millie has more work and Mister Engstrom could use Manny, so I'm here t' home alone. Mister Cameron, do yuh think Millie should work at Flora's house?"

"No, I don't, and I don't think she has to, Lou."

"Mister Jervis makes me feel creepy now. He didn't useta."

"Reckon you're growin' up. When will Millie be home?"

"In a little while. How long kin yuh stay?"

"Most of today, then I'll ride up to Wells Creek

tomorrow. Want me to say hello to the Klingers?"

"Yeah—and tell 'em I'll come see 'em someday."

22

DYER'S DUCKING

DUST FILLED MILLIE'S shoes as she walked home
after a day of cleaning house and baking for Mrs.
Warren that had brought her fifty cents. When she
saw the fresh tracks of a shod pony in the sandy
soil, her heart leaped. Near the cluster of buildings, Buck drowsed in the shade of cottonwood
trees, his saddle blanket hung on the garden fence.
Millie forgot her weariness. Her need of Cameron
had its way with her and she wanted to run to
where he was, hear his slow drawl as he rolled a
brown-paper cigarette.

"Well, look who's here!" she said. "Has Lou talked yer ear off?"

"Millie, it's good t' see yuh. I'm gonna stay a little while. Lou says yuh got green corn—hope she hasn't fed Buck my share. Take a dip in the crick and I'll help her get something to eat."

In the garden, Louisiana and Cameron gathered the corn and some tomatoes. They had a fire going when Millie came up the path from the river, bright hair gathered high on her head. Cameron breathed faster when he looked at her.

"I feel some better now," she told him. "When we was livin' south, there was jist sand an' horny toads. It seems like heaven here by the river where I kin swim iffen I want. Land, you an' Lou got enough garden stuff fer two families."

"These tomatoes sure are fine—the first I've seen around."

"Missus Warren started 'em in a cold frame. I ain't tasted 'em before, but I like 'em. She had me can some already."

"Millie," Cameron smiled down at her, "here's a little package from Mister Denny."

When she saw the comb, brush, and two ribbons for her hair, Millie clasped them to her breast, bit her lips, and hurried to another room, overwhelmed by Denny's thoughtfulness, his gift an expression of the love and attention she and Lou craved.

After their meal, they went outside in the dusk and watched the light fade over distant hills. Quail called along the river. The heat left with the sun, and coolness came to the land. A little breeze rustled the cottonwood leaves, and an old mallard hen quacked from a slough across the water. Cameron sat alone with Millie while Lou went to milk. He could not see her face, but her soft accent was clear.

"Thank yuh fer sendin' Mister MacClure t' see us and help us, Mister Cameron. I know now what it is t' pray t' God. Things're a mite easier."

"I wish you'd call me Percy," the cowboy put in.

"Percy . . ." She hesitated. "It means somethin' t' me to have yuh t' talk with 'bout things. Reckon it give me stren'th. I could stand work an' heat long as I had Paw an' Loper—now all the boys is gone. Funny, ain't it?"

"Reckon it is. Me, I took off on a high-headed pony early in life, missed bein' around women a little, and then got weaned. But when I head your way I feel like I was comin' home to somebody."

Millie moved toward him. "When I seen pony tracks in the sand, I knew yuh was here. Everything changed right then."

Cameron's arms came around her and she leaned close against him. He bent his face. The bright hair was there. He closed his eyes, holding in his clasp everything he really wanted.

The sharp point of a dry moon broke over the Raggeds and rose slowly until its silver shape might have served to "hang a powder horn on." Would it ever rain in this arid land of sage and sand? The river was low and warm.

Finished milking, Lou fed the calf and closed the chicken house door. Buck nickered softly at her as she passed him on her way to the house. Lou heard Millie say, "Percy, I wish yuh luck. Don't fergit t' tell Mister Denny thanks."

"That goes fer me, too," Lou said, stepping close.

Cameron smiled. "Don't let Engstrom keep Manny away too long. Your Paw wants yuh to find a place to homestead. I can help with that. So long, girls, next time I see yuh don't feed me so much. Never wanta leave if yuh do."

"I'll walk down with yuh, Percy." Millie paced with him toward the cottonwoods. "It's cool now. Next month'll bring frost, then winter. Where'll yuh be then?"

"Not far from here, if my plans work out. Boss said he might have a new job for me. Buck, yuh old hay-burner, have a good rest?"

Cameron threw on the blanket, smoothed it down, and lifted the heavy saddle. Buck grunted as the cowboy pulled up the cinch, but he opened his mouth for the bridle bit. Cameron flipped out rope, coiled it in quick motions, and tied it at the horn. He gathered Millie close, patting her shoulder. "Don't worry, girl. Take care of the kids and your paw." He swung up, and Buck trotted out the lane.

As Millie walked back to the hovel she called home, she drew a long breath. Cameron had her trust. Crickets sang in dried grass along the garden fence. Lou was in bed when she reached the hogans, and Millie lay listening to night sounds until sleep came.

Tom Dyer was surprised to see Cameron enter

his office again. The cowman's approach was blunt. "Well, sheriff, yuh figgered who murdered the Blecker boys yet?"

"Keep out of it, Cameron! You ain't hirin' me!"

"My outfit is. They pay big taxes an' may pay more."

"Hell of a lot of other people pay taxes, too. I got other things t' do besides run all over the country on one wild goose chase."

"Listen, Dyer. I've been checkin' up on what you've done in office and there ain't one damn thing that amounts to a whoop in hell. From what I hear you're about as useful as a wart on a pig's nose. Come next election, any young feller with a gift of gab can run for sheriff here and win."

"What do you bullheads expect? There's more t' this job than yuh think."

"Like inspectin' Flora Miller's girls?" Cameron's voice cut. "The sheriff and marshal at Carson said yuh hadn't been there to consult with them since the boys' murder. The letter you wrote 'em laid things out so doggone far from what actually happened that yuh oughta be kicked out for writin' it, let alone sendin' it to honest law officers."

Dyer slumped back in his chair. The expression on his face reminded Cameron of a trapped meadow mouse. His eyes slithered back and forth, his lips curled, and beads of sweat appeared above his brows.

"Dyer, why don't yuh quit coverin' up your part in this affair and figger out how the skunks left alive can be caught and hung? That won't be easy and you'll hafta double-cross one or two of 'em.

But hear this—if yuh don't help hang 'em, they'll help hang you! Savvy?"

"Cameron," Dyer whined, "yuh got me mixed up with somebody else. Yuh come bustin' in here givin' me a song and dance 'bout bein' crooked an' mixed up in murder, when yer jist a cowpoke canned fer spendin' too much time with a crazy man's red-haired daughter. Hell, it's all over town—" His words died away in a gurgle and crash.

The cowman leaped over the desk, his hands to Dyer's throat, and the sheriff crashed back on the floor, struggling for breath. Searing agony struck as a hard knee came up between his legs.

Cameron got to his feet, pulled the groaning sheriff outside to the watertrough and heaved him in. When he pumped more water over him, the sheriff jerked erect, gasping and gagging, floundering like a carp in a flooded meadow. Across the street, Ben Jervis walked out on the store porch. Above the Bar Nothing a window was pushed up and women's heads poked out.

Blacksmith Jery Dean came around the corner. "What in hell goes on here?"

Cameron was laughing. "The sheriff had a fit. Jumped around like a Mexican bean and fell into the trough. I come along and pumped in more water. That right, Dyer?"

"Yuh, yuh, yuh—Dean, this roughneck jumped me in my own office, kicked me in the belly an' slung me inta this trough. I'll file charges!"

"Go ahead, Dyer. It's your word against mine. Dean, this feller is plumb nuts. He acted like a skunk-bit dog, rolled his eyes, frothed at the mouth, then fell in the trough."

When Dyer stumbled into his office and slammed the door, Cameron looked at the big blacksmith and winked. "Dean, the county needs a new sheriff. I reckon every stockman around would back yuh to run against him."

Dean was astounded. Was this ramrod of a big cow outfit suggesting that he, Jerry Dean, run for sheriff? "Think I'd have a chance?"

"Why not? You're honest, you're a smart, strong feller, yuh know ranchers and farmers, yuh got a family, and yuh go to church. It's time somebody halfway decent got in."

"I'd do it if you'd back me. How do I start?"

"Set still—I'll mosey around and see people, stir folks up. Size up the job and listen to what goes on. Talk with MacClure, the new preacher."

Jervis saw the sheriff crawl out of the water-trough, sputtering and gasping, watched Cameron talking with Jerry Dean, and wondered. The cow-man crossed the street and his booted feet clomped on the store porch.

"If it ain't Cameron! Been outa town?"

"Yeah. Say, how long has Dyer been nuts?"

"What yuh talkin' about? He's allus been all right around here, far as I know."

The cowman leaned on the wooden counter and rolled a smoke. "When I asked him how his investigation of the Blecker boys' murder was comin', he said he was workin' on it, then went off on a tangent about how well the Blecker girls'd do in a fancy house, and how you was setting Millie up for

Flora. When I told him he was crazy, he r'ared back, his eyes rolled in his head, an' his tongue got blue. I did the only thing I know to cure fits, dragged him out and dumped him in the trough." Cameron gave the paper a lick, looked at the finished cigarette critically, and stuck it in the corner of his mouth. "The blacksmith come along and Dyer told him I was pickin' on him."

Was Dyer trying to save his own skin? Jervis was in a cold sweat. Maybe Flora Miller had double-crossed him when the sheriff was there on inspection. "Beats me, Cameron."

"He mentioned yuh knew more about the Blecker killings than yuh let on, said you an' the old bitch over the saloon were thicker'n fleas on a hound dog."

"The lyin' bastard's cooked his goose. He keeps talkin' that way an' crazy er not, he won't last long. Somebody'll shoot him."

The two men fell into more casual conversation, each trying to read something from the other, as they talked about what was going on around the country. When Cameron left, Jervis was a worried man.

At the bar, Jake greeted Cameron. "What's fer you this early, buckaroo? Beer? Whiskey?"

"Beer, Jake. Thanks for your help the other morning."

"My pleasure. Saw the sheriff takin' a bath jist now. Must be purty dirty t' jump in with his clothes on."

"Had a fit, Jake. Plumb crazy. Said things about Jervis and Flora bein' in cahoots, that Jervis knew more'n he lets on about the Blecker murders, then he got choked up and fell on the floor. I've cured many a cur by dumpin' him in water. Sure worked on Dyer."

Cameron drank his beer.

"Feller name of Jack Logan comin' in to see me, Jake. Got a room we can use? Big deal on for Jack's cows."

Jake showed Cameron the room reserved for card players in a private game for high stakes. It had no windows a man could sneak up to and shoot through. After sizing it up, Cameron thanked Jake and walked upstairs to Flora's rooms.

At his second knock, Flora called out, "Too early to do business!"

"It's Cameron. I won't take long."

"Okay, Cameron. You alone?"

"Yeah."

Flora opened the door, her hair in curlers above a bright-red wrapper; she had been drinking coffee and looking over old magazines. She filled a cup, shoved over a bowl of sugar, and motioned for him to sit down. "Well, cowboy, what's on yer mind?"

"I'll have a crew comin' through long about first of October, I reckon. There'll be at least ten buckeroos. Boys ain't been out on a tear fer awhile an' they got money to burn."

"Yuh wanta see the new girls? Drink yer coffee an' I'll have 'em come in the parlor."

Flora led the way. In the red-draped room, she turned to the new girls. "Ming, show Mister Cameron what you look like."

A delicate-looking Chinese girl not more than

fourteen years old rose, turned awkwardly, and dropped her gown. Cameron was shocked at her emaciated body. She appeared half-starved, ribs showing, her pelvic region fleshless, buttocks palm-sized handfuls. After that first glance, he looked only at the fragile bone structure of her face and her slanting eyes. She trembled. Another Chinese girl, not much older, stripped casually and with an almost insolent smile made her bow front and back.

They were the first Oriental women Cameron had ever seen. In low tones, Flora told the watching cowboy of each girl's specialty.

"Flora, I like redheads. What yuh got in that line?"

"I might have a new redhead later on."

"Must be the one Dyer was talkin' about."

"The sheriff?" Flora stared. "Girls, go back to bed if yuh want."

"Hell, maybe it's a secret," Cameron said.

"What'd the old possum-belly have to say?"

"Spoke about you an' Jervis dealin' for a redhead. Made me want to come up."

Flora didn't like to think Cameron might have found out about her scheme. People knew too damn much now about how she did business. "Come back in October and see," she said.

After Cameron left the saloon, he found MacClure unloading foundation stone hauled from the river. The preacher hailed him. "Put your horse in the shade, boy. I got a job here for a strong back and big hands."

"Mac, sure looks like you're gonna have that

firm foundation people sing about. It's good to see someone with gumption around this town." Cameron dropped rein and began throwing rocks off the wagan, noting MacClure's brown-red sweating face, his hands rough with calluses and cuts.

The stones unloaded, they sat in the shade while Cameron told of visiting the Bleckers. MacClure confirmed the story of Flora and Jervis's scheme to trap Millie. "Percy," he declared, "I thought I'd find reliable men in this town, but Jervis surprised me. We're up against difficulties in trying to get enough decent souls together here."

"Flora's bought some young Chinese girls," Cameron replied. "Mac, we fought a war to free the southern slaves. Should people be able to buy and sell human beings in this country? For all I know, it's legal, but I'd like to look into it. It'd be the only way I knew we could break Flora. If women in this town knew their men're gonna see Chinese women . . ."

"Percy, maybe I can come up with an idea."

"I'll be around the Bend for some time yet. Let me hear—and keep the Bleckers happy."

That Saturday in the Bar Nothing, Cameron and Jack Logan faced each other across a table in the private cardroom, drinks between them.

"Art an' I figger we kin bunch three hundred head of young stuff," Logan said. "There's yearlin's, and some heifers that'll be in perty good flesh by fall. I reckon the lot should be worth fifteen thousand."

"I hafta see 'em first," Cameron told him. "I

can buy four hundred head of fat steers from a fellow has a ranch up on the South Fork for twelve dollars a head, gathered, right now, or get his whole ranch for Denny for seventeen thousand, includin' twelve hundred head of stock an' all his horses. That makes your price seem kinda high.''

Jack Logan was dumbfounded that Denny would have seventeen thousand dollars to put out just after being robbed. The Ajax must really be a gold mine! ''Cameron, you sure Denny wants to buy that spread?''

''Sure am. I got an option right here for Denny t' sign when I see him. I'm due to show it to Levi Esch at Willow Springs, too. Levi's a friend and business partner of Denny's. You could see him about a deal with Denny anytime.''

The more Logan drank and asked questions, the keener he was to possess the Ajax. Before their meeting broke up, he allowed that Cameron could advise Denny or Levi Esch that he might trade his ranch holdings for the mine—cattle, horses, land, everything except two ponies and their rigging. Cameron went to bed that night almost too pleased with himself to sleep.

23

LOGAN SCHEMES FOR THE MINE

JACK STAYED AT Flora's that night, slept with
Mexia, and didn't get up until late next day. After a
breakfast of sorts, he saddled his pony and rode
out of town, heading east toward the distant hills to
the trail that led to the Ajax. He saw no recent
tracks, and rode close to the cabin before he called
out. There was no answer. The Ajax was deserted.

He looked over the cabin's contents, sorted ore,

gratified to find flecks and streaks of gold all through it. He picked up a candle, lit it and walked to the very end of the dark, dripping tunnel with its rubble from the last shot, convinced now that old man Denny had a real gold mine. He collected some pieces of good bright ore to take along. Jack Logan was ready to deal, to swap his ranch for the Ajax or sell it and buy the mine.

At Willow Springs, he asked Levi Esch if old man Denny would consider trading his mine for the Lazy L and five hundred cows, twenty head of horses, and whatever else was around the place. Levi played dumb, and said he thought Denny was looking at a piece or two but really wanted a spread along the river, the south fork, maybe, where he could irrigate for crops.

Jack reminded Levi about the creek and springs on the Lazy L. A man could winter many cattle there by irrigating the meadows and putting up hay. But Levi seemed uninterested. "Denny told me he'd taken enough gold before this last shipment was stole to last him the rest of his life and had it in the bank," he said. "I figger he made at least ten thousand a year. He never talked much, but allus pays cash fer anything he buys."

"Jesus, Levi, he sure fooled me. He lived like a dern packrat."

"Denny can back up a deal, all right. How'd you get into this?"

"You know Cameron. Him an' me talked about cattle. I set a price on this fall's gather, then Cameron showed me a ninety-day option on a ranch that he'd put together fer Denny—seventeen thousand, cash, lock, stock an' barrel."

"Whew!" Levi whistled. "I happen t' know that ranch was priced four thousand more'n that a month ago. I reckon a drop in beef is due."

"Why's Denny gettin' inta it, then?"

"He's a miner, don't know no better. All he knows is gold."

"Esch, why can't I swap my layout fer the Ajax? If Denny buys that ranch, he'll still have the mine an' nobody t' work it. If he really wants t' git rid of it, why don't he deal with me?"

"Jack, I'll approach the old man," Esch told him. "Are you authorized to dispose of the Lazy L? What about Art?"

My brother Ed died not long ago, I kin deal Art out of his share."

"Well, better get Art to sign an option while he's still livin'." Esch paused, staring at Logan. "Denny won't touch a deal unless it's clear," he went on. "How about your titles?"

"We bought out Jackson and each of us homesteaded on a spring with a hundred and sixty. We claim all the land that Jackson had. What makes yuh think Art could kick the bucket?"

"I know a lot of fellers died of lead poisoning this summer. Your brother Art's a pretty rough customer—travels with fellers I wouldn't write insurance on. Sooner or later he'll end up dead."

Logan let the reference pass, and asked, "What's this about Tom Dyer goin' bughouse? I said somethin' about it t' Dyer an' he liked to run me out of town."

Levi Esch laughed. "Cameron dumped him in

the horse-trough when Dyer had some sorta fit.
Jerry Dean was there, too. Looks like we need a
new sheriff.''

"Dyer'll see to it nobody runs against him.''

"Things change, yuh know. Dyer's in deep. Say,
yuh tried out Flora Miller's new stock?''

"My gawsh, Levi, one o' them slant-eyes is
skinnier than a wet white-poke an' the other smells
like rotten fish!''

Jack went back to the Lazy L. Art Logan and
Kit Welch rode in next day with an antelope they'd
shot, and roasted the loins over a pit of coals. Jack
brought out a bottle of whiskey. While they drank
and feasted, the great idea came to him: he and Art
could claim their dead brother Ed's share of the
stolen gold. Welch had one share, but the shares of
the two dead men would have to be divided three
ways. If Welch could be eliminated, with thirty
thousand dollars in the stolen pot, he and Art'd
have fifteen apiece. If Art would sell him his half of
the Lazy L for about seven thousand, Jack could
trade the ranch for the mine.

"Art,'' Jack began, waving his tin cup of whiskey, "what'll yuh take fer yer share of the ranch?''

"Who wants t' buy it?''

"I do.''

"Where the hell yuh gonna git enough cash t'
buy me out?''

"Wal, lessee now. Stock included?''

"All 'cept a couple ponies.''

"Seventy-five hundred in gold.''

"Make it seven thousand even.''

"Okay! Gold—no silver er treasury notes.''

"Yuh heerd him, Kit. Now, you fellers know dern well if we all go t' pick up that gold in Carson we'll land in the jug. I guarantee t' cash in yer gold fer one-third of it an' take all the risk."

Art Logan slumped back and eyed his younger brother.

"Boys, I don't really want this dern ranch. It was jist a headquarters when Ed was alive. I got a deal started t' swap the Lazy L fer old man Denny's Ajax Mine. I'm gonna run that mine, take in the Ajax ore we got now, bring back the money in my name an' split with you fellers. Savvy?"

"My God, it might work." Kit looked at Art.

"An' where yuh gonna dig up seven thousand fer my share of the ranch?"

"You'll git it outa my share of the ore."

"Then yuh'll own the mine all by yer lonesome, and we won't git nothin' but what we stole?"

"If yuh set an' wait, yuh might even git a rope around yer neck er a hide full o' holes. There's a feller Cameron that's poison, an' he's got a big outfit behind him. He dunked the sheriff in the horsetrough, told off Jervis, got Flory stirred up, an' let people know one robber was tattooed. So far, he don't have no idee I was in the scrape."

Kit Welch looked down at the tattooed arm. There was a long silence.

"All right, Jack, git the papers made out—I'll sign the ranch over t' yuh."

Art wrote a statement giving Jack his share of the ranch. They tallied the stock on the place and dug up old papers showing Jackson's titles and claims. It was near morning when they got to bed.

Jack rode in to see Levi Esch, who had knowledge of titles. He looked over Jack's papers, then suggested, "Jack, get this witnessed by somebody knows both of yuh. That way, you're in the clear if anything happened to Art."

"Can you be a witness, Levi?"

Levi pondered a moment. "I could. If Art's at the ranch now, I'll take a rig an' ride out."

Esch had more than one reason for going to the Lazy L. He wanted to size up the layout for himself and take a good look at Art Logan and Kit Welch. On a rough table in the ranch house, he spread out the documents. "Well, boys, this looks all in order. Title . . . deeds . . . list of properties. Kit can sign as witness too so's I won't be the only one if somebody hollers fraud."

"Okay—here's our turkey tracks."

Levi put the signed papers in his carpetbag to record in Hooper's Bend next day. As he rattled down the dusty road in his rig toward town, Kit turned to Art. "I got a funny feelin' we better pick up an' git."

"Hell, Kit, Levi ain't gonna talk."

"Mebbe so, but I think we better pull freight. I sure don't want no posse to ketch me."

Jack nodded agreement. "You're the ones got pecker holes in your hides."

"Soon as we git located we'll let yuh know where we're at." Art led out his speckled packpony. "So long—an' git started on cashin' in that gold."

Jack watched them ride west. A half-starved cat came meowing to the porch and he kicked her out into the yard. "Take that, yuh noisy old bitch! I own this place now!"

But Jack knew his problems. It would soon be time to round up cattle, cut out salable stock, move bulls to the meadows, then scatter the cows onto wintering grounds. Ponies must be fed and gotten ready for the gather. He needed good ranch hands; of the crew that used to work the Lazy L, three were dead and buried, two headed west. Only himself left.

Riding along, Levi Esch grinned like a fox who had found a dead horse. What Cameron had in mind would work. Jack had the ranch, and would end up with the mine. By spring and green grass, somebody would begin to try to collect on the ore at Carson City.

Sick of Carson City, smelters, lawyers, and the eternal squabble there over mines, money, and women, Bill Denny made up his mind to head for Hooper's Bend and his mine in the Raggeds. He caught the night stage.

Rufe Bledsoe drove into Hooper's Bend toward evening. He had a message for the Bleckers. When he turned the stagecoach onto the river road, Lou heard its rattle and was outside when Rufe pulled up at the house.

"Lou, here's a letter fer yuh. The feller sent it is on his way here."

"Thanks, Mister Bledsoe. If yuh see Mister Cameron, jist say we're all right."

"Save me a kiss, Lou. Giddap there, Dick an' Dan! So long, kid." Dust rolled as the stage turned and vanished through the brush.

The letter was from Mr. Denny, who had stopped over in Willow Springs and would come to see them before long. He would like to board with them, he said, until he got straightened around.

Bill Denny and Levi Esch, old friends, ate supper together, then went to Levi's room. Denny first said he'd been told by Cameron that a couple of cowboys who might work for Logan were coming through on the next stage. Levi brought out Logan's papers and they sat down to examine them, discuss the ranch's value, and how the deal could best be consummated.

"Bill, if I was you I'd play hard to get. Go see the Bleckers, go up to your mine, make a visit to Voss, let it be known you're takin' your time. Jack's already got the itch to trade or buy. I've found out they're the ones got the ore. They want your mine so they can cash it in legal."

"I trust Mister Cameron, Levi. If he'll handle the ranch and cattle like he says, a half interest in it for him would be cheap. He'll earn it many times over. This deal won't cost me a red cent. I wouldn't have dreamed it if I smoked opium for ten years!"

The old trader laughed, then sighed. "I wish I was younger and had Cameron as pardner. It makes me feel younger to listen to him, watch him operate. I'll bet he makes BMT more money than any other man on the payroll."

"Mister Blake told me Cameron could have a share of the BMT anytime he wants it," Denny observed. "You two work it out. I want to get the ranch legal, and cheap as possible."

"Cameron'll see to that. Look up the new preacher in Hooper's Bend while you're there. Cameron says he's all right. Check with the sheriff, too. He may be sore enough to talk. Things have been pretty rough for him lately."

Two buckeroos, their saddles in gunnysacks, got off the morning stage from the south. They were looking for riding jobs. Levi Esch loaned them a rig and gave them directions to the Lazy L. They seemed decent enough; Levi thought that when Cameron brought in his riders, the Lazy L might have an honest roundup that fall.

Mr. Denny didn't get off the stage in Hopper's Bend, but stayed inside until it wheeled up to the Blecker hogans. Lou ran out in time to see Mr. Denny climb down before the vehicle turned back to the main road.

"Lou, yuh look good."

"We got yer letter. Sure was surprised. How come yuh want t' board with us?"

"Gettin' old an' lonesome, I reckon. Millie in town?"

"Yeah, she's workin' fer Missus Warren again. Have yuh seen Mister Cameron?"

"No, but I seen Levi Esch. He sent his kind regards—and here's somethin' special I brung yuh."

In the package was a complete outfit—dress, stockings and shoes. Lou cried with joy, as she held the dress up to her. "Oh, Mister Denny, I'm so happy I jist cain't hold it in. Never had nothin' so perty in all my life."

The old miner smiled. Lou did not see the tears

that glittered in his eyes.

When Millie came home, Lou ran from the back of the house and Millie looked in surprise at her sister, dressed and beautiful in city clothes. Mr. Denny stepped out to greet her with a package that held everything Lou had received, plus an elegant whalebone corset. How had he ever managed to buy such a thing and all the rest? Millie would never know that a high-class madam in Carson City had loaned him a girl to shop with him and try things on for size. Denny knew no other women.

Manny's box was placed by the door until he returned. The group watched him untie the cord. He pulled out a black, wide-brimmed hat, a buckskin jacket, checked shirt, a pair of Levis, and cowboy boots. He tried one of them on and felt something in the toe. When he shook it, a Barlow knife with the "Sheffield, England" mark fell out. In the other boot he found a red neckerchief like the one Cameron wore. Manny said nothing, but as he took his new clothes and went out, Millie saw his upper lip tremble. When he came back he was dressed every inch a real cowboy proud to be looking for a job.

24

NEW LIFE AT THE LAZY L

CAMERON HEADED NORTH from Hooper's Bend, stopping at several ranches to buy cattle on his way to Duck Lake, where in the course of conversation he managed to relate the horse-trough incident, and to ask in innocent surprise if anyone had known the sheriff to have "fits" before. As it made the rounds, the story spread, and by the time Cameron had reached the Wells Fargo stage stop it had enlarged beyond his expectations. "If we had an honest feller like Jerry Dean in office," he declared, "we wouldn't have these hold-ups and killings. He's a dern good blacksmith but he'd make a better sheriff."

Greeting Cameron warmly, Mr. Klinger immediately took him to see the mules. He had reason to brag. Mose and Maisie were having the time of their lives in a sort of mule heaven, with kids to ride and drive them, and bring them stuff from the garden. Klinger made it clear he'd gotten the best of the deal. When Cameron told him about the murder of the Blecker boys, the wrecked wagon, and the pony needlessly killed, the old German stormed.

At Duck Lake, bulls fattened in the meadows, and on grassy flats a herd of cows had good winter browse. Cameron began setting up a crew of men for a late September gather at the Lazy L Ranch.

Ben Jervis really stirred things up when next he visited Flora. She accused him of blabbing to Dyer and to every wandering miner or cowboy of how she did business. Ben knew someone had talked. It must have been the sheriff. He hastened to Dyer's office.

"My God, Tom, how come yuh told Flora I said she was makin' a play for Millie Blecker an' spilled the beans about me bein' mixed up in that hold-up?"

"What in the name o' Moses yuh talkin' about, Jervis?"

"Dyer, yuh talked too much t' somebody. You'll lose yer job when your hook-up with that Logan tribe comes out. The sheriff at Carson's lookin' fer two fellers with buckshot marks—one with a tattoo on his arm. Now what all did yuh tell that buckeroo about me and Flory an' the Blecker girl?''

Dyer came out of his chair. ''Nothin', Ben, I swear it. It was when I said somethin' 'bout him an' a crazy man's red-haired daughter that he come up like lightnin' an' nailed me.''

Jervis had to accept the story. But how had Cameron found out about Flora? ''Dyer,'' he said, ''we gotta stick together an' keep our mouth shut or we're dead ducks. Cameron's up to somethin'; mebbe found out more'n he's lettin' on. You talked with any o' the Logans?''

''Not since that day both me an' Cameron was both out t' the Lazy L. Jack never come in t' tell me 'bout his confab with the cowboy. By God, Ben, we might have trouble.''

''Yuh better figger on gettin' rid of him, Tom, legal if yuh can.''

After Jervis left her, Flora Miller saw him go into Dyer's office, and sat where she could watch, knowing things were serious when he did not emerge for an hour. Trouble for him meant trouble for her. She rocked, waiting for night trade from the ranches.

Reverend MacClure wondered what kind of a town he had come to. Wild and rough, good and bad people in this community. Each had a different problem, each a different outlook. He suspected Dyer the sheriff of being a four-flusher and double-dealer, and he knew now there were many persons who profited in devious ways from dealing with him, some belonging to the church. He alone could not close Flora Miller's place or force her to leave town. Men and women of the community would have to put on the pressure. The preacher planned strategy while he built a church, hoping for changing times in Hooper's Bend.

When the two cowboys off the stage came riding into the Lazy L Ranch in Esch's rig, they found Jack sitting in the shade, playing solitaire with his worn deck.

"You Jack Logan?"

"Yeah."

"Man named Levi Esch at Willer Springs said yuh could use a couple riders."

"What yuh countin' on?"

"Fall an' winter work."

"Forty bucks an' chuck here. 'Course yuh'll hafta take turns burnin' the biscuits. Yuh kin hang yer hats an' start right now."

"Suits me, Windy. Whaddya say?"

The smaller cowboy nodded and a fleeting smile crossed his face.

"Okay, I'm Nevada, Logan. Yuh jist hired a couple sage-smellers."

"I got 'bout a thousand head here to gather next month," Jack explained. There's a deal comin' up to trade this ranch, but if yuh take to it yuh kin stick right here fer the new owner. He's an old coot but a perty fair feller, I hear."

Jack showed the men where to put their warbags. The team was unhitched and put in the barn, and Nevada and Windy walked to the corral to choose mounts among the ponies dozing in the shade there.

That afternoon they started on the pasture fence, driving a team and wagon as they spliced and tightened wires and drove in loose posts near the creek. At the lower end of the pasture a bunch of horses stood switching flies and dozing. Both men noticed a long healing scar high up on one gelding's flank.

"Lead," grunted Nevada. Windy grimaced agreement. "Hell, they could herd antelope on them ponies. That dried blood on one o' them saddles in the barn is sure a tip-off." Windy nodded, a frown between his eyes.

Jack Logan didn't get far with Levi Esch. Levi told Jack he'd seen Denny and tried to talk about a deal, but the South Fork rancher had lowered his price for cash. But he supposed Denny would come and look at the Lazy L.

"Jack, if I was you I'd clean up that place," Levi expanded. "Denny's not a rancher, he's an old bachelor miner, likes things clean and neat. Go see that Waldecker family at the edge of town— they're existin' on little or nothing. Let the woman cook and scrub the joint and have the old man outside reddin' up and gettin' rid of junk. They got a kid'll help, too. If it passes inspection I'll bring Denny out, try to sell him on the deal."

"Yer crazier'n a bedbug, Esch. What does cleanin' up the place have t' do with sellin' it?"

"It might mean the deal. Clean, it'd be no chore to take over the work. No man with money'll move

onto that place as it is. Jack, yuh gotta horse-trade.
Fix your fences, repair the bunkhouse, buy some
whitewash.''

"Levi, yuh may be a Jew but I guess yuh talk
sense. Then again, mebbe yuh got a cut comin'.''

"If you get the mine, I'll get the orders for your
powder and I'll handle your ore shipments,'' Esch
said bluntly.

"Well, I'll git on my way, and take yer advice.
But if this deal falls through, I'll come in an' shoot
yuh, Levi. Hear that?''

"Yes, I hear. I'll meet and raise yuh. If the deal
goes through you pay me one hundred dollars in
gold.''

"Hell, a hundred bucks! Why, yer crazy!'' Jack
realized he had said just too much.

"No, I ain't, Jack. You want this deal. Now put
up or shut up.''

25

PERCY AND MILLIE

PERCY CAMERON HAD yet to gun down a man. Growing up in rough midwestern towns, he had had the usual scrapes with youngsters. After a bloody one, his farmer father would say, ''Boy, yuh cain't go on this way. The way to avoid trouble an' fights is to keep ahead of the game, half-kill the other feller quick as yuh kin, tear him apart so fast he won't have no time t' think. The word'll git around that you're poison. But don't fight lessen you're in the right an' kin win.''

All men carried guns on the western range. Percy had started early to practice with his Remington. As days, weeks, and years went by the gun became merely an extension of his pointed finger and he shot by feel and instinct. Riding for an outfit down in the Territory when he was twenty, he saw gunfights, and a few men killed. On the trail with Brownie, another cowboy, one day they had come on a sharp-horned bull on the prod, a maggoty rip along his ribs irritating him to frenzy. Cameron figured they could rope him, then clean him up a little. At the moment Brownie's rope looped the bull's horns, his horse stepped on a rattlesnake. The pony whirled twice—his rider was caught. Percy pulled his gun and without thinking or sighting shot the rope in two close to the bull's head. When Brownie told the story, he always said, "Good thing Percy's a nice easy feller to git along with 'cause he's too fast with his gun fer anybody around here—don't fergit that!"

When Rodney Black wanted a ramrod for the BMT, Cameron had been suggested. BMT wanted a man in new territory to have the respect of all cowmen and homesteaders. Cameron had a reputation for not only avoiding trouble but being able to stop it, once started. The best way to prevent range wars, lawsuits, and stolen beef was to have such a man represent the BMT Cattle Company.

Many a rider was convinced Cameron was crazy when brands were disputed at round-up time and their boss waved the mavericks out until the whole herd was worked. Cameron looked the critters over. If there was reasonable doubt, he would say,

"Slap a good iron in right now so it'll never happen again." After a round-up or two there were fewer disputes and ranchers soon learned that BMT played fair and they could depend on what Cameron said.

Now Cameron rode south, happier as he went. Rumors he had heard concerning Dyer and the Logans made him feel confident the end of his quest wasn't far away, and he had begun wanting to acquire more so as to offer Millie more than a saddle job with a cow company. As he splashed through the ford, he saw the first yellow cottonwood leaves afloat in the shallow water. Soon be time to round up cattle for the winter grass at Duck Lake. He smelled smoke, and wondered if Millie was home from town yet, wanting to see her and hold her again.

Manny was at the bend, trying for trout, when he heard iron-shod hoofs strike rock. He pulled in his hook, wound up the line, and started down river with his string of trout. Milking the cow by the garden fence, Lou heard the gentle thump of hoofs and saw the buckskin's high head. Her heart bounced. Mister Cameron was coming. Millie, just home from town, had bought beef, a roast and some steak, the first they'd had in months. She heard the rattle of wheels, Cameron's "Whoa now!", and ran to the door to see her cowboy, dusty and unshaven, at the side of a buggy drawn by a sleek red-and-white pinto pony.

"Millie, can a saddle bum get a meal here?" Cameron called. "I got somethin' to swap for it."

"Percy . . . I been lookin' fer yuh. Where'd yuh

git that beeyootiful pony an' buggy?"

"Klinger. Him an' me decided you kids could use another outfit like this."

"Mister Denny's stayin' with us. Manny, give me the fish an' help Mister Cameron with his horses."

"Manny," the cowboy said, "Mister Klinger sent the pony to you an' Lou. His name's War Cry, but when he acts up they call him Little Skunk."

Lou struggled up with her brimming bucket. "Mister Cameron, ain't he a beauty?"

Millie set the milk pail in the house and put the trout in a pan before she returned to Cameron. "How's yer paw?" he asked.

"Same as last time. Say, the whole town's talkin' at how yuh dumped the sheriff in the horse-trough. Mister Denny said yuh should have did it long before. There's lots o' news. We kin talk after supper. Will yuh have steak er trout? Reckon yuh better choose fish—it's so long since we had steak I might ruin it. Mister Denny brought me an' Lou new clothes from the city. After supper I'll dress up fer yuh."

Swept by love and tenderness, Cameron looked at her, bright hair loose around her temples, the rest gathered and tied with a blue ribbon. He wanted to take this wide-eyed girl in his arms and squeeze her so tight she couldn't breathe.

"That would be the nicest thing. . . ." He paused. "Say, how about me taking a swim in the crick before supper? I'm dusty as a tramp."

"Why, go ahead. Mister Denny'll be here pretty quick. Percy, let's take a walk afore it's dark t'night."

"Been lonesome?"

"More'n that for me." Cameron sighed. "Got it bad, girl. Never reckoned it'd hit me, but I guess I'm a goner."

"Goner! Are yuh sick?"

"Never mind, we'll talk later. Get the fire for that steak goin' while I clean up."

With Mr. Denny and Cameron there, everyone was happy, and that night seemed like a family reunion. They talked of the Klingers, Sheriff Tom Dyer, and of Jack Logan's interest in swapping his ranch for the Ajax.

Millie fed her father and Lou and her brother did the dishes while Denny and Cameron walked outside. Cameron rolled his brown paper cigarette and together they sat on the cottonwood log.

"Percy, we might have a cattle ranch one of these days. You're the boss. What d' yuh have in mind? Jack'll be gettin' me out to the Lazy L before long."

"Bill, don't promise him nothin'. Look over the layout and sorta turn up your nose. Say yuh'll pay cash for what yuh want. He'll talk trade. Tell him the mine's no good, ore's run out, the good vein's pinched off. The more yuh tell him it isn't worth what the ranch is, the more he'll want to deal."

Mr. Denny chuckled.

"Play it the way it's laid out and yuh'll get his cattle—horses, too."

"How about help on the place?"

"There should be two fellers there to stay on. Of course yuh already figgered on the folks here movin' out there. Manny'll make a hand in a year or so and with you and the two girls there to see everything runs smooth and the riders keep their saddles polished, it won't take more. I'll cut the herd down to easy feedin' this winter and pick up a few bulls for the spring work.''

"With you around it'll all work out, Percy." Denny sighed. "The girls want to show off their new clothes. Wouldn't dress up for me—that's the hell of gettin' old. Let's go see."

In the bright flare of the new lamp Mr. Denny had brought, Millie and Lou were resplendent in their new clothes. If Percy Cameron thought of Millie as pretty before, he knew she was beautiful now. Her hair piled high, the strings of her fashionable corset pulled tight, she looked mature, a woman grown. Cameron's surprise turned to delight.

That night along the river, the moon high over the Raggeds, a breeze stirring the leaves of the cottonwoods, Millie and Percy walked down to the water, sat on a log and talked about the future. She wondered about Mister Denny and how long he would be with them, what they would all do when winter came. Would Bill Denny go back to the mine?''

"Millie," Cameron's arm was behind her, "I didn't want to say anything before, but I better tell yuh now what we figger on. Denny and I are tryin' to get the Logans' Lazy L. Jack Logan's already told Levi Esch to make the deal, trade the ranch for the mine. We want you and Manny and Lou to move out there to live with Mister Denny. The kids can go to school in the Springs.''

"It sounds too good to be true, Percy. But what

about our paw? I reckon he'll never be any better.''

"Take him along. It won't all be a bed o' roses, but it's sure gonna be better'n you got here. By spring I reckon I can come up with another proposition if yuh still think yuh can put up with me.''

"Percy, I kin put up with yuh fer a great long time. Why do yuh do so much fer us? I never could've made it this summer without yuh.''

"Girl, let's figger ahead. Better think of movin' soon. If our deal goes through, I want yuh out there right quick.''

Millie trembled against Cameron's arm and he wondered if she was cold. "No—jist excited. I ain't gonna be able t' sleep at night. How big is that ranch?''

"Darn near as big as we want t' make it. There's not much deeded land. A lot of it's held by right of use and that's where we can handle more stock. There's supposed to be a thousand head under the Lazy L brand but I doubt if they're all legal. We'll winter at least three hundred head and bring in new bulls in the spring. From then on, watch our smoke!''

Cameron tightened his arm and pulled her close. Millie turned her face to his and he put both arms around her, feeling the crisp softness of her hair beneath his cheek. She tipped her head back and before he really knew what he intended, Cameron was kissing her.

That kiss from Millie Blecker wasn't the practiced kiss of dancehall girls he'd known. Millie's kiss was light and gentle at first, a caress offered, a promise of love and trust to be given. She knew her own need, and sensed his confident response as he pressed her closer to him and sought her lips again and again.

26

JACK PERSUADES DENNY

LEVI ESCH DROVE Mr. Denny out to the Lazy L
Ranch behind his team of trotters. The two men
looked for signs of cattle in the sagebrush. Mr.
Denny had dreamed of owning a farm or ranch in
his time. If Jack Logan wanted to deed the Lazy L
to him for his hole in the ground, Denny decided he
would take the offer—that is, if Percy Cameron
would ride the range for him and the Bleckers
would move there and keep house. He wanted to
be free to enjoy his last years.

"Bill," Esch told him, "land they claim lies clear to the road. It's just good for winter feed. Back where you see yellow cottonwoods under the rim is headquarters. The ranch runs another ten, twelve miles west."

Esch was amazed at what had been accomplished at the Lazy L since his last visit. Fences were fixed, all the manure spread on a spot to be a garden, porch boards replaced and windows repaired. The place looked like a working ranch. Mr. Waldecker and his son were working on a bunkhouse door, on its porch was evidence the interior had received a coat of whitewash.

Jack came out, shaved and cleaned up, wearing a new hat, vest, and boots, shiny spurs jangling.

"Jack, this here's Bill Denny," Esch greeted.

"Git down, Mister Denny. Yer jist in time fer dinner. Got a dandy new cook. Harry!" he called, "Take the team inta the shade. Mister Denny, I heerd yuh was lookin' fer a ranch."

"Yeah, I am, but mebbe I'm wastin' your time, Mister Esch's too. I have the offer of a spread along the South Fork."

"Hell's fire! Well, it won't hurt t' eat dinner an' talk. Want a drink o' whiskey?"

When they sat down, Levi saw that the rickety furniture had been replaced with a new table and chairs, cookstove and dishes in place, a rug on the floor, all new glass in the windows. Mrs. Waldecker, neat in her calico, brought in bowls of food, giving the men a good meal while they talked weather, beef, mines, scandal—anything that came up.

"If yuh sell out, what're your plans?" Denny asked Jack.

"Yuh might not believe it, but if I kin find me a mine, I'm going' minin'. My brothers Art an' Ed are gone and it don't make no difference t' me. I'm gittin' out."

Esch put in his word. "I told Mister Denny yuh might be interested in his gold mine, Jack."

"Jack, you wouldn't be interested," Denny said quickly. "All it ever brought me was grief an' trouble. I took a little gold and I made a fair livin'."

"Well, some gold mines I know of never took out any a-tall. If yuh made a livin' an' saved up enough t' git inta ranchin' yuh musta did all right."

"You have a point there. I don't think I want to get rid of it, though. I can still piddle around minin' in the summers."

"Mister Denny, jist what d'yuh want in a ranch?"

"Plenty of water, some flat ground I can irrigate if I want close to a town, and not over a day from the mine. I'd like to have space fer five hundred to a thousand head of cattle, with some stock already on the range."

"This place'll fill the bill a lot better'n most in these parts. Lots o' water, good summer feed, best winter range this side of the line. A fast pony kin make it t' Willer Springs in half an hour, no bridges t' go out, no rivers t' cross. But it's everyone to his likin'. Wanta ride over the layout an' look at the stock an' grass, Mister Denny?"

"I don't know, Jack. I have a good cattleman

friend who'll look over your place for me. I can see the headquarters and the buildings, but I can't judge the rangeland. When he comes over to the Bend, I'll have him come out here and stay a few days. Mr. Esch'll let yuh know."

"That's fine, Denny. We're gonna start the round-up in a couple weeks. Cameron of the BMT Cattle Company is buyin' three-four hundred head o' young stuff, but if you an' me make a deal I'd call that off."

"Cameron's gonna buy your stuff? Hell, he's the feller I had in mind to look the place over."

"Jack, why not ride along? You ain't in any big sweat, are yuh?" Levi asked.

It was the last thing Jack Logan wanted to admit. Denny grinned at his answer. "Hell, no if I do make a deal with Denny I'd jist end up a-swingin' a single jack in the hole and a-bustin' my knuckles."

Cameron chuckled when Denny told him about the visit to the Lazy L. The longer Jack sweated over it, the easier he would be to deal with.

In a few days, Mr. Denny and Manny Blecker drove the new buckboard and pony out to the Lazy L Ranch. Cameron was there with six riders and a wagon to help in the round-up. More work had been done on fences and barns, and the manure on the garden spot had been plowed under.

Jack Logan appeared. "Well, Denny, are yuh in a swappin' mood t'day?"

"Might be."

"Cameron an' me been talkin'. I'll swap yuh the

232

ranch, free an' clear, twenty head o' ponies an' their riggin', cattle up t' one thousand head, fer yer mine an' the ore on the dump. I can move out soon as the cattle're tallied."

"Jack are you serious? You'll swap straight across?"

"Cameron says it's a good deal. From what he knows o' grass, the ranch'll carry a thousand head."

"We'll make the swap," Denny declared. "But my God, yuh don't know nothin' about minin'. I hope you'll be satisfied."

Jack hailed Cameron. "Come on over fer witness! Denny, we'll shake hands on it. Don't worry about me an' the mine. The Ajax's gonna be worth it!"

It took five days to round up, sort, and brand cattle from the Lazy L range. Cameron ran the outfit. He sized up stock for age, condition, and quality, wanting to pick five hundred head of cows, a bunch of the best heifers, and two hundred steers. . . . Cattle of every description streamed in from the high grass flats, from under lava benches and along little creeks and basins. Manny tallied at one fire, Denny at the other; cows, bulls and steers Cameron wanted on the place had a D slapped on them above the Lazy L. Doubtful brands went into the BMT cut along with the culls and saleable steers, the BMT brand burned on their left ribs.

On the fourth day they made their trip across the valley, riders scattered on their ponies to comb high ridges and little pockets. Cameron saw grassy meadows, small lakes, potholes, and ridges under the pines where grass still stood brown in the sun, and knew he wanted this summer range for his best cows and bulls.

When the round-up was over, Jack Logan was paid for two hundred and eighty head over the thousand agreed on in their swap. Cameron wrote out checks: one to Jack Logan, the other to Denny for what the BMT took, and had Jack sign a paper that held him responsible for any kickback on altered brands.

It began to rain. Summer was over, a new season about to begin. Cameron left orders with his men where to take the BMT stock, and turned back toward Hooper's Bend. He had a few things yet to straighten out, a trip to make to Carson City. A cold raw wind blew up the river as he rode into the Blecker place. Tying Buck under a shed, he walked to the house, stripped off his slicker, and whipped the rain from his hat. "Hey, anybody home?"

Millie came to the door, her face withdrawn and sad. "Millie, maybe I come just in time," he said.

"Yeah . . . I'm all alone and I reckon I'm lonesome. Mister Denny an' the kids is over town gettin' papers fixed up an' buyin' things. Percy, are we actually goin' t' live on the Lazy L and not hafta worry 'bout money no more?"

"It's honest-to-God-true, Millie. I come by to see yuh an' make sure everything's legal before I leave fer Carson."

"Yer wet an' cold. Come on in by the fire—I'll

234

start the coffee. How 'bout somethin' t' eat?''

''Fix what yuh want, Millie, and eat with me. How's yer paw?''

''Reckon that's really why I was lookin' sad. Doctor Marsh from Dayton come t' see Paw. We cut the hair around the bad place on the back of his head. The doc said he couldn't help, but if he'd seen Paw right at first he might have. It's too late now, he said.''

''Millie, that's sure too bad.'' Cameron's face twisted. ''Things'll be better all around when you folks git moved to the Lazy L. Anyone around the Bend know you're goin'?''

''I reckon they all do. I told Mister MacClure yuh would manage the ranch. Did yuh know Flory Miller's got two Chinese girls up there over the saloon now? I'm glad I never went t' work fer her. I kin see Mister Jervis was up t' somethin', tryin' t' git me to.''

''What do Lou an' Manny think of movin' out to the Lazy L?''

''Manny says it's wonderful—Lou, too. Will yuh be at the ranch sometimes?''

''Yeah . . . you'll see me around there.'' Cameron watched her move from table to stove. ''There's good meadows, buildings are fair, and I seen a nice place to build a new house some day. Good garden already, and lots of water.''

By the time Denny and the kids returned, the meal was ready, and while they ate rain poured down steadily, soaking through canvas and sod to drip on the floor, but it was warm inside. The cowhide door flapped open now and then to let in a spray of moisture. Early in the afternoon, Cameron rode off in the easing downpour.

When Ben Jervis heard that Mr. Denny had swapped the Ajax for Jack Logan's Lazy L Ranch, he knew he'd been double-crossed. He walked across to see Tom Dyer.

"Tom, yuh know damned well Jack sold us out. He's gonna take that ore an' claim he mined it. We cain't do a thing about it. How he pulled the wool over his brother's eyes beats the hell outa me."

"Let's lay low an' see what happens, stay outa things till the smoke blows away."

"I don't agree with yuh, Dyer. Time goes on— first thing yuh know we ain't a-gonna have no share a-tall. I think we better jump Mister Jack Logan. We got somethin' comin'. I think he give his t' Welch an' Art fer the ranch, then swapped the ranch fer Denny's mine. Do we jist sit an' howl at the moon?"

"Jump him if yuh want. Yu'll end up with a cold chunk o' lead in yer gizzard."

"You gonna sit an' take it?" Jervis spoke with controlled fury.

"Cain't do otherwise, Ben. I see trouble ahead. That cowboy started things now built up too big t' knock over. Flory's got her tail in the air like a heifer in fly-time. Even Rousty Collins won't say a good word fer me anymore."

"If someone'd plug Cameron we might pull outa this, Tom. Would Jack have the guts t' do it?"

"Yer crazy. Yuh know what'd happen if yuh

asked Jack t' do sich a thing? He'd tell Cameron—upset yer wagon. He ain't t' be trusted by us no more. But get this—I'll bet when Welch finds out he's been screwed by Jack, he'll be ready to knock off Mister High'n-Mighty."

27

AMOS BLECKER'S DECISION

CAMERON RODE BY MacClure's house. The
preacher invited him in, introduced him to his
wife, then took him into his small study. Percy
brought the other man up to date on events, even
mentioning Doctor Marsh's visit to the cap'n.
They discussed an investigation of the Chinese
slave-girl racket. The two agreed that before long
it would be time to talk to Jerry Dean in Tom Dyer's
place as sheriff.

When Cameron reached Willow Springs, Levi Esch told him that Jack Logan had given him a hundred dollars to see the ranch deal through, confessing he felt he was almost stealing the mine. Doctor Marsh had stopped for the money Cameron had left for him and given Esch a letter for Percy Cameron, which confirmed Millie's account of his diagnosis and said that the captain would gradually get worse until he was no longer able to respond at all.

It was bad news. Cameron stood at the window, musing. "Levi," he said finally, "can yuh find three hundred tons of hay around here and have it hauled to the Lazy L this winter? Pay half down, the other half when we holler and it's delivered." The old Jew nodded. Cameron turned to look at him, adding, "I wouldn't be surprised if somebody made a play to kill me or Jack Logan. Keep yer ears to the ground."

"You must be lookin' for a rough winter."

"I own cattle now. I want 'em fed. And I wanta stay alive. I'm headed south to pick up a set of bulls for the ranch. You'll meet the Bleckers when they come through, movin' to the ranch. Levi . . . the oldest girl is mine."

Esch stared. "Allus wanted to tell her 'bout buryin' Loper," he said. "Okay . . . the hay . . . Jack Logan's health . . . the Bleckers. See yuh when yuh come back."

Cameron cut across country to the Lazy L once more and found Jack going through personal things. The two men sat by the fire with a bottle of whiskey. "The Bleckers'll be movin' in next week," Cameron said. "I'm headed for the assay offices at Carson and Virginia City to show 'em a letter from Denny sayin' the Ajax Mine is legally yours and you've taken over."

"Thanks, Percy. Don't worry about things here. Windy an' Nevada're perty fair hands."

In Carson City, Cameron was told that no one had yet come for the assay and money due for the stolen gold ore. The sheriff had a hold order on it; the mine trade would not affect this gold stolen before any deal was made.

The storm had put snow on the high Sierra. There was frost in the valleys. Cameron chose twenty bulls from three different ranches, red Herefords with white faces. He thought he might select a few of his top cows and start a herd of his own with them. After he had made arrangements to hold the bulls for a few days until he could start them for the Lazy L to winter at the ranch, he saw Rodney Blake and told him the whole story of the Lazy L, the mine trade, the Logans, and his own furture hopes. Blake wanted him to stay on with the BMT at a salary and let him run the outfit in the time he could spare. When they parted, Cameron's mind was at ease.

Over Hooper's Bend, skies cleared and the temperature dropped. Next morning white frost covered the ground. There would be a few warm clear days, each one shorter than the last. The Bleckers began preparing to move to the Lazy L. Mr. Denny and Manny went to the lumber yard for boards to build up the wagon and make a pig crate. Millie stayed to talk to her father, who had come to that morning and eaten a good breakfast. When he asked who had cut his hair, Millie told him a doctor had been to see and examine him.

They talked again of Cameron's help with the mule trade and how he got the Jersey cow and the new pony for them. The ranch deal was news. Mr. Denny would hire her and Manny and Lou to help him on the ranch, Millie said; they were getting ready to move out there in a few days. They'd all be better off—mabe he'd get better, too. She looked out and saw that the cow had broken her picket rope and was loose, headed down the river. Asking her father to stay where he was, she picked up a rope and ran down toward the flat.

In his lucid interval, Amos Blecker thought seriously how he could make things easier for his children. He knew he was a drag on their progress, Millie's greatest worry, a burden for the future. He found a pencil and wrote two notes, one to his family, the other to Denny, then dragged himself into the other room, found one of his old pistols, loaded it and said a short prayer, lay down on the bed, held the gun to his temple, and pulled the trigger.

Millie had trouble catching the cow and leading her back. Driving in the picket stake, she thought she heard a shot but when she looked up she saw no one. She tied the cow so she couldn't pull loose, then stopped at the garden to survey the frost damage, pick ears of corn and carry them to the pigs. When she got back to the house, almost half an hour later, she found her father dead. Powder fumes lingered in the air, and in the darkened room she saw blood on the bed, dripping on the floor. "Oh . . . Paw!" she moaned. "Oh . . . Paw . . ." She knelt beside him and took his hand. Tears of anguish flooded her eyes. In a few minutes she rose, pulled a covering over her father's body, and settled herself beside him. As soon as Mr. Denny and Manny came back she would go and ask Mister MacClure to help her make arrangements to bury Amos Blecker.

Mr. Denny read the note left by him by the cap'n.

> Dear Friend:
> I trust you will not resent this action of mine. I believe it's the best way to help everyone. There's no hope for me, I know. By taking my own life now, I will make the children's life easier. Bury me close to my son Loper in Willow Springs. You and Mr. Cameron will see to it that the children are settled and looked after for a few more years. I have nothing to leave to them but my blessing and hopes for their future happiness.
> Cap'n Amos Blecker

He's better off, Mr. Denny thought, *and so are his children. I owe it to him to see they're taken care of, for it was my gold that got three of his boys killed.*

In the buggy, Millie drove to the MacClures, over her first grief, thinking now of her father's burial, the trip to Willow Springs, and moving their stock to the Lazy L.

The MacClures listened and agreed as she told them what had happened and what she wanted to do. MacClure would make arrangements for burial the next day in Willow Springs. They could have an early ceremony here in town and the family could then drive to the grave site. He had time to get a note to Levi Esch, asking him to have a grave dug alongside of Loper's.

Jack Logan had once seen Millie Blecker from a distance before she had grown up and filled out in front, but now when she stepped down from the buggy at the Lazy L ranch she was a real looker, and Jack wondered how he had missed her. He busied himself outside until time to eat. Millie put an apron on and got acquainted with Mrs. Waldecker. During dinner, Jack told the Bleckers he would move what few possessions he had left up to the mine next day.

While Mrs. Waldecker and Millie washed and dried dishes, Lou helped unload their meager household belongings. Manny and Harry Waldecker took vegetables from the wagon to the root cellar. Waldecker hopped from one place to another, his main object being to keep far enough away from his wife so he wouldn't have to listen to her constant stream of talk.

"You know, Millie," she ran on, "it sure seems good to have a woman to talk to. I think Mister Cameron's a fine man. Is he sweet on you? You don't hafta answer—I know he is. He comes in here last trip through, saw the old closet out back 'bout t' tip over, an' he say t' the mister, 'Waldecker, pull that thing down, cover the hole if there is one, an' fer gosh sakes build one close t' the house, fer the wimmen.' Well, it ain't been used yet. I made Waldecker plane down the rough edges an' when he made a smart remark I bashed him on the head with a board. Yuh know, I seen that there Jack Logan sizin' yuh up. He's got wild blood in him—wild idees. Takes after his brother Ed what Jack buried out there by the red-leafed tree. When I cleaned up around here I found bullet holes in the house an' a shirt with a hole in it, blood from one end t' the other. I went ahead and burned it. They musta had some high old time in this house.''

Mrs. Waldecker looked slyly at Millie. ''S'pose yuh heard of the new Chinese girls in Flory's place. The mister says Chinese wimmen're different, their privates is cross-ways, slanted same as their eyes. I told him if he ever went t' see, I'd fix him with the cleaver some dark night. Do you believe that trash?''

Millie had to answer, but she avoided Mrs. Waldecker's look. ''A lady friend said it ain't so.''

''Jack told the mister if they'd fatten them slant-eyes up a little he'd git one fer a cook up t' the mine. All they eat is rice an' dried fish.'' Mrs. Waldedker turned to the bread, now risen, ready to be kneaded down. Millie found small things to do so that as she worked she could listen to Mrs. Waldecker's never-ending stories and news. It kept her mind off her father.

Percy Cameron rode in two days later, having stopped in Willow Springs where Esch told him of Amos Blecker's death and burial. ''Percy, I liked them younguns," Levi said as Cameron paid him for the hay. "Girls like Millie're scarce as hens' teeth in this country. Now that some of these young fellers know her father's dead, they'll be after her."

"When we get married, Levi, I'll invite yuh to the weddin'," Cameron chuckled. "I got a few things to clear up first, though." He rode off, urging his buckskin. When the horse tried to slow a little, he got the prick of spurs in his flanks, and kept a steady gait. In sight of the ranch buildings, Cameron let him take it easy just to get the feeling of riding into his own place where the girl he longed for waited. Horses in the meadow tore down along the fence, their tails in the air like flags at the sight of the buckskin. Millie noticed and knew who was coming.

She hung up dish towels and combed her hair, selecting a blue ribbon Denny had given her. Rascal barked outside, and Mrs. Waldecker's thoughts ran on, silently for once. "When a girl puts a new ribbon in her hair, she's got somebody she loves comin'. Never saw a girl purty as Millie. Reddest hair . . . and bluest eyes. If I was Mister Cameron I'd jump off that claybank an' squeeze her till she hollered yes. An' if I was Millie—oh, shoot, woman, yer too old t' think o' that no more. Iffen yuh ain't keerful, the mister'll wonder what ails yuh t'night."

"Millie," said the cowboy, "you're the nicest thing I've seen since last I saw yuh."

She smiled. "Ever'body's out lookin' at the cattle. Kin I walk down t' the barn with yuh t' unsaddle Buck?"

"Sure thing." His hand brushed her shoulder. "Levi told me about your paw—and the burial. That musta been hard. But yuh sure look like you've gotten over the worst."

"I'm a-feelin' better. Maybe it ain't right, but soon as Paw was gone I felt better. I could think, and make my plans."

Cameron looked down at her. What could he tell her but the truth? "Millie, it has t' be that way. Lots of folks might think different, but the old gotta give way to the young. Like with the Injuns—an old squaw might give out on the trail, wrap her blanket around her, and just wait for death to come. Many an old Indian buck has walked out in the dark or storm so the rest of the tribe had a better chance to survive."

In the cool light of the autumn day they looked at each other. "I've missed yuh, Percy."

His voice lowered. "I want yuh more all the time."

Her hand sought his. "How long yuh goin' t' be here?"

"Few days, anyway."

"Could you an' me take a ride tomorrow? Yuh could show me the whole ranch."

"Let's figger on it, take along a little grub. I'll show yuh country yuh never knew existed. Ever been up in the Raggeds?"

They sat in the kitchen and had coffee and pie. The comfort and pleasure of it reminded Cameron that Millie and Mrs. Waldecker should have plenty of food on hand for stormy weather. Cattlemen would drop in from time to time, and no one was to leave the Lazy L without being offered a meal and room in the bunkhouse, he told them.

The sun was low when Millie and Cameron walked out again. "Where should we build the new house?" Cameron asked.

"Do we need a new house, Percy?"

"Sure do. When we get married, I don't plan on livin' in that old place. Need a brand new house fer us. You pick the place and we'll get it started."

She stopped and faced him. "Are yuh sayin' yuh want us to marry, Percy?"

"Yeah." He smiled. "Ain't that what you want?"

"Oh, it is . . . but I hardly dared t' think of it."

His eyes held her eyes and swept over her luminous hair. "We'll figger on six rooms to start with. That spot over there's shady, handy to water, and far enough away from the barns an' bunk-house."

They spent an hour looking and planning, every existing building examined for its value and im-provement possibilities. Cameron found that this girl who had lived in a covered wagon and in a set of hogans not much better than those of the Digger Indians, had good suggestions and practical ideas. He knew how to locate corrals, gates, and cutting chutes and that barns were for convenience, not looks. But he took time to analyze what Millie had to say. He now had a partner.

Next day on top of the ridge, they sat in heavy grass at the edge of the pines while their ponies rested and they ate their lunch, looking east into the sage desert.

As they talked on their plans, Cameron held her in his arms. Millie told him what she remembered of her mother, how her father had left for the war, and how they had managed to survive for four years after her death, until their father returned. When his injury became worse, they packed up and headed for California, hoping they might find gold, and ended up in the tangle of makeshift buildings near Hooper's Bend. Cameron knew most of the rest of their story.

He held her close, kissing her again and again until she forgot her tears and responded. There under the trees they decided they would have Douglas MacClure marry them in their new house at the Lazy L.

28

JACK LOGAN TRIES HIS LUCK

AFTER JACK LOGAN moved to the gold mine and
started looking over samples from which to pick
high grade, he realized he'd jumped into something he knew little about. The stolen "gold" in the
Blecker kids' bag was far from pure, and the costs
of assaying and smelting would run high, he sur-
mised. He knew that meant that the difference
between gold smelted down ready to coin and that
in the coin might be great, and their haul would be
less than the gang had figured on.

He hired two Mexicans—the boy Pedro, and Gonzalez, a tough drifter. They hauled up and wheeled out ore from rubble in the mine's depths. When Jack tried to sort it for color and weight, the magnifying glass only confused him; but just as he was about to give up, he would wash a sample, see a bright speck of color, and go back to sorting once more. The old man had tried to follow the vein, working side pockets and ups and downs—so would he. Still, ranching and rustling had never looked quite so good to him as when he woke up one morning to four inches of snow on the ground, more coming. The tunnel would be warm; the Mexicans wouldn't feel the cold. They could not be trusted to work out on the dump—they'd steal him blind. At that moment, he would have sold the Ajax Mine cheap.

He called Pedro and Gonzalez in, told them to keep drilling, then load and shoot. He was leaving for a few days; when he came back, he'd help them clean up. There was grub in the cabin, and inside the tunnel they wouldn't notice the cold and deepening snow.

In Hooper's Bend, Jack got drunk, spent the night in Flora's place, and headed south for Carson City on the stage next morning. The weight of his baggage over the thirty pounds allowed cost him twenty-five cents a pound, but if he wanted to haul what he had in the bags, he had to pay for it.

In Carson City, he squabbled over assay reports and smelter returns. He didn't get enough money out of the whole deal to pay off his brother Art. "Mister Logan," Watson said, "yuh think this ore is gold and figger the price yuh git paid is like for pure quill. It ain't. Top o' that, yuh got to pay me an' the smelter. When yuh take your ore to the smelter where little jags like yours are a headache, they make a quick estimate, deduct what they think the traffic will stand, pay you off, and your ore's dumped in with a charge for one o' the smelters. If you don't like it, what can you do? How'd yuh ever happen to buy out old man Denny in the first place?''

By this time, Jack knew he was a sucker. "It was a swap deal, but let's not go inta that. If you was in my boots what'd you do with that mine?''

"Start lookin' fer a bigger sucker.''

Jack collected what money was due him. Going over every angle, he came up with but one thought: how could he recoup? The other two would kill him if they suspected a double-cross. His brother Art would be hell on wheels, and Kit Welch would want to knife or shoot Jack Logan.

He made the rounds of the dives and places of entertainment. All he heard was news of mines and all sorts of lucrative speculation: everyone who knew anything about the business had an optimistic story to tell of wealth being uncovered. Logan began to be convinced once more that if he worked it right maybe he could come out ahead with his mine after all.

Ben Jervis had watched Logan argue with the stage driver about his extra heavy baggage. Jack must be taking gold to Carson City. So far, neither Jervis nor Dyer had been approached by anyone connected with the robbery with an offer to settle up and divide the loot. After an hour or so, when trade slacked off, he went across the street to see the sheriff.

"Tom, Jack Logan left for Carson with too much baggage. I'm damn certain he had fifty, fifty-five pounds of ore. Figger it out. When he comes back with the money, you an' me better ride up to the Ajax, see what we have comin'."

"What's he done with Welch an' his brother? Kin yuh answer that?"

"No. Hell, yuh don't s'pose he bushwhacked 'em, do yuh? They was s'posed to've gone to Texas, remember? That'd make Jack Logan the sole survivor. He's cut us out, cut the bunch down to hisself."

"Ben, what yuh tryin' t' tell me?"

Jervis shrugged. "We ain't been paid off, Risk and Thompson're lyin' in the desert, and Ed Logan's dead. Art and Kit Welch've just plain disappeared. Jack swaps the ranch fer the Ajax. Who's t' say he cain't git rid o' the gold an' do it legal? Jack's turned out smarter'n all the rest of us."

"Whaddya figger we oughta do?"

"Wait till he comes back, then ride up to the mine and call fer a showdown."

"S'pose he bucks?"

"Then we better figger on gittin' rid of him. I want my split!"

"Get ready t' kill then, 'cause he won't give in easy 'thout a rope round his neck er a gun in his belly."

San Francisco passed an ordinance making it

unlawful to: ". . . sell, or attempt to sell, any human being; to claim the services, possession, or person of any human being, except as authorized by law; to solicit, persuade, or induce any person to be or remain in a state of servitude, except as authorized by law, whether such person receives partial compensation or no compensation; to be, enter, remain, or dwell in any brothel or house of ill fame, except for lawful purpose, on account of any real or pretended debt due, or pretended to be due, by any person, or any passage money paid for, or money advanced to any person, whether in this state or elsewhere; to hold or attempt to hold the person, or claim the services or possession of any human being except in cases authorized by law; to exercise control or attempt to exercise control over any human being."

White Christian men and woman were determined to stamp out the importation and slavery of Chinese women and girls. The purchase price rose at once from fifty dollars at Canton per person to one thousand dollars in San Francisco for the more desirable and attractive females. Dupont Street and St. Louis Alley, main places of illegal trade in the city, were under constant watch by the authorities. People were interested in where slave girls were taken and held as prostitutes. Armed with this information, Douglas MacClure sounded out his congregation. Would they want the Chinese girls removed from Flora's place, and have it closed down completely, forcing Flora to leave town?

He found various reactions. Some men were for getting rid of the whole outfit, others just the two

Chinese girls. Quite a few laughed, and said, "Hell, Parson, let well enough alone. What Flory does is nacheral. Been goin' on fer thousands o' years. Yuh cain't change human nature."

Douglas MacClure wrote to San Francisco acquaintances. Would someone come to Hooper's Bend and lecture on the evils of the slave trade and what could be done? He would combine their facts with an attack on vice in the town. He was quickly assured that two ladies would make the trip.

Indian summer drew a close. Snow topped the high mountains, and game dropped to lower elevations. Every night's frost spurred builders and harvesters to greater effort. MacClure's church could now be completed inside in the bad weather. Opening services would be held the first day of November. At the Lazy L, the new house was up, first fires laid in its fireplaces to help cure the rocks and mortar. Mr. Denny and the mister, as Mrs. Waldecker called him, spent most daylight hours sawing, planing and fitting. The smell of pine lumber wafted through the empty rooms. Each day Millie went to see, listing things needed to furnish her new home.

Denny had not forgotten his mine nor the stolen gold. Jack's having the Ajax didn't alter the fact that men had been killed, that sooner or later criminals must come to light and judgment. Cameron had gone north to Duck Lake; when he returned, the wedding would take place. But old man Denny had a feeling there would be more trouble before Cameron and his bride settled down.

Once Jack Logan left, the two Mexicans

speeded production. Pedro and Gonzalez had the idea that if they worked fast they could drill the face, load it, and shoot before Logan returned. If the shot opened a new vein, they would look for color and steal the best ore. Working around the clock in the dark mine, the two pounded steel, changed bits, sweated and drove deeper. While one made a fire and cooked a meal, the other manned the forge, heating and shaping drill bits. Then with renewed energy they took candles and reflectors and went back to the rock face. Two days before they expected Jack, they loaded the holes and placed fuses.

Riding the stage, Jack Logan tried to reason away his fear, but the closer he came to Willow Springs the more certain he was of danger ahead. He stepped out in the late afternoon with his small bag, slipped the driver a gold piece, and said, "If anybody at the Bend asks if yuh saw me, yuh didn't." He went into Levi's place. Levi had his hostler get a saddlehorse ready while Jack ate and changed into heavier clothes. It would be dark when he reached the mine, snowy and cold. He paid Levi. "I'm slippin' up t' the Ajax. Far as yer concerned, I ain't back yet, though." Levi nodded. The sounds of Jack's trotting horse died away.

Logan hit snow at the first bench. Crossing open places he saw no tracks but as he approached the cabin, his nose told him someone was cooking supper, and that a shot had been made in the tunnel. Powder smoke drifted down in the cold air. Tying his horse, he walked soundlessly, approaching the cabin from behind. He made little of what the two men talking in Spanish within said—the shots, ore, tomorrow's exploration. Logan returned to his horse and rode up the trail in the dusk.

The two opened the door at his holler, jabbering, helping with the horse, telling him they'd worked like hell, lost track of time. Jack pretended he was right on schedule, ate supper, and asked about the shot. They were waiting until the shaft cleared of fumes before investigating, they said.

In the morning they all went into the rubble-filled tunnel. Here and there the lights picked up glitter and Jack took samples. Outside, he said, "Boys, yuh kin go in t' town a' have yerselves a time in Flory's. Here's half yer money—when I come in tomorrow or next day you'll git the rest. Savvy?"

"Si, si, Señor." Jack handed each a gold piece, and the grinning pair headed down the mountain. Jack went to the ridge to watch the trail until he was satisfied they were well on their way to Hooper's Bend.

In the Bar Nothing, Jake served each Mex a drink and answered their questions. They would have a few drinks, then go play with the señoritas. Mexicans with money to spend were not plentiful around Hooper's Bend and word of their presence spread.

Flora was ready for them, her girls out on parade. In the middle of the week trade was light. She wanted all the money they had. They talked to Mexia in their own tongue but were more interested in blond Heinie and the two Chinese girls.

They began to argue over choices, chattering away. Flora asked Mexia to find out how much money they had. Mexia smiled and sat on Pedro's lap, wriggling, feeling along his thighs, putting her hands in his pockets like a curious child. Before he could protest, she had something to look at. Flora saw it, too, and made up her mind to somehow get the small chunk of rock gleaming with gold away from the sixteen-year-old Mex.

The Mexicans stayed two hours, and left promising to come back next night. Flora said she would furnish the drinks. She had one chunk of gold but she knew Pedro had a larger one; it would be easy to steal it from that snot-nosed kid.

Jervis learned from Flora next morning that the Mexicans had rough gold nuggets as well as money. They told her Logan had hit it rich and that they would get a share. Mexia had arranged for them to come back that night to play with the Chinese girls.

Ben Jervis saw Tom Dyer, insistent on setting out that afternoon after Jack, before he left the country or cashed in all the gold. Dyer reluctantly assented.

Sounds of horses' shoes on rocks in the trail below the cabin alerted Jack and he slipped outside to wait for his visitors. The sheriff tied his horse under a tree. "Jack, it's Tom Dyer an' Ben Jervis!" he hollered. "We come up with a little news."

"Yeah?" Logan's voice was even, cold. "Better

come in the cabin while we talk.''

"Wait a minute, Tom, till I get this cayuse tied.''
Jervis was cool and collected. "Don't wanta hafta
walk back. Jack, we heard this mornin' yuh was
here.''

The men walked to the cabin. "Yuh fellers like a
little grub, I reckon.''

"Sure, Jack.''

"Set still. I kin fill up the stove an' git the coffee
goin' while yuh tell me what's brought yuh up
here.''

Dyer started the talk. "Well, your Mex boys
come in town loaded, spent some time in the
cathouse. Besides money, Flora come up with a
chunk o' gold. We was wonderin' if yuh knowed
the boys was passing around gold.''

"They had a chunk, eh? What'd yuh figger it
was worth?''

"Maybe twenty-five bucks.''

"Nugget?''

"Nope. Piece o' quartz, white granite around it.
Been broke off a stringer someplace. Up here, I
reckon. Yuh been passin' out samples?''

Jack stiffened. He had seen a line of white
quartz in the tunnel at a place he hadn't examined
closely. Was it the vein again?''

"Nope. Guess the fellers had it from
'nother job. Hain't seen nothin' like that up
here—yet.''

"Me and Dyer wanta know what kinda deal yuh
made with the other boys about the gold the gang
got, and where we set in the deal now.''

"If I remember right, it was you tipped Dyer off

about the shipment and it was Dyer tipped Ed off. Ed made a deal with you fellers. That right?''

"That's right, Jack—go ahead.''

"We was t' git the box from the kid. Dyer was sure nothin' would happen. Well, the kid didn't bluff, an' he got his guts blown out. Fifty pound o' ore in that box. Welch took it to Carson. Stupid bastard—he left it in his name. It's still there. Either of you fellers want it, go ask the Watson assay office.''

Dyer and Jervis glanced at each other.

"Then Ed tells me you come to him in a big hurry, Tom, said that Ben told yuh the Blecker boys was haulin' another load o' gold to Carson. Ed sent me ridin' t' make sure the boys was on their way. We was t' split the take seven ways, one share fer each of us six, you an' Ben the seventh. And what happened?

"We stopped 'em. Ed got a pistol bullet right in his gizzard. The kid with the shotgun got Risk the first barrel, Thompson with the second. Buckshot nicked Art and darn near ruined Welch. But we killed the kids an' got away. Ed died—he's buried on the ranch. Risk an' Tommy're buried out in the desert. I reckon yer itchin' t' hear what happen t' the gold, how Art signed away the ranch, an' I got the mine. Hold yer fire—here goes.

"I made a deal t' buy Art's share o' the ranch fer seven thousand bucks, cash, then traded the ranch an' cattle t' Denny fer the mine. Why? 'Cause you stupid bastards never told Ed we couldn't cash in the gold ore without signing where it come from. You gotta have a mine to cash in gold ore from it. I told Art and Welch I'd cash their share of the loot in fer one third. Here's where you fellers come in. You'll git paid off from Art and Welch when they git theirs. I made that a part of the deal an' there's nothin' more you bastards kin do about it!''

"Like hell, Jack! You maybe bushwhacked them an' all the rest and are settin' on the whole caboodle! Come up with somethin' better'n that er it'll be too damn bad fer you!''

29

GUNFIGHT AT THE AJAX

"HOLD IT, BOYS!" came a voice from the door.

"Well, if it ain't the rest o' the gang!" Art Logan and Kit Welch looked grim, guns cocked and ready as they entered. The small room suddenly seemed hot and stifling. Jack kept on slicing steaks from the deer haunch he had ready. "There's plenty fer you fellers, too," he went on. As the knife cut the fibers, and Jack dropped the slices into a hot skillet, Welch's mouth watered.

"Well, Jack," Art said, "how much money yuh collected from the ore?"

"I took a little jag in from the tunnel last week for workin' an' eatin' money," his brother replied. "The stuff Welch took is still there. I ain't about t' cash it in till the coast is clear. Jervis an' Tom come up t' jump the gun."

"Jack, yuh know damn well why we come. The Mex come t' town an' flashed gold around—Jervis an' me ain't never had a smell of any. Just set us straight on what's goin' on an' we'll lay low till the last dog's hung," Dyer whined.

Tension filled the room. Half-turned, Jack saw Welch's gun still out, held low as Art Logan stared at Jervis and the sheriff. He pulled the coffee pot to one side. "Coffee's done, steak soon will be," he said. "Pot o' beans simmerin' on the back. Fill yer plates anytime."

"These bastards're lookin' fer trouble, Art," Welch said.

"Aw, steady down, Kit," Art replied. "Let's eat, then talk things over. Got any bread, Jack?"

"Yeah, there's Mexican sourdough in that round can."

The men filled tin plates and walked to the table, the whole group on edge like a bunch of strange dogs, violent action easily set off among them by any sudden noise or movement. Art ate his steak, finished a cup of coffee, and stepped to the stove to refill his cup.

"Jack, how much did yuh git fer the jag o' ore?"

"Little over four thousand bucks. Smelter an' assay took more'n I figgered."

"How long 'fore we git some gold?"

"Don't see much chance afore next spring."

"Next spring! Yuh bughouse?"

"I'm layin' off the two Mex, goin' south fer a spell. Things're gonna git hot here, an' it'd pay us all t' git out."

Art stopped, cup to his whiskered mouth. "Why's that?"

"Ever hear of a feller named Cameron? He's got the country all stirred up 'cause the Blecker boys' murders wasn't solved. Gonna elect a new sheriff 'fore long. Cameron's got a lead on who tipped us outlaws off t' the gold, they know Art an' Kit was shot, and they're lookin' fer Ed's grave."

Jervis jerked erect. Dyer choked on the meat he was chewing. Only Kit Welch remained cool, black eyes squinting. "Leaves yuh holdin' the pot, don't it?" he said.

"I jist missed jail by the skin o' my teeth," Jack told him. "I traded the cows with the ranch, even the blotched brands, and I got me a mine so I kin cash in on gold you fellers helped steal. Set tight, I tell yuh, an' take no chance—yuh'll all git paid off."

Art Logan slurped his coffee, wiped his mustache. "Ben, yuh got anything t' say?"

"I heerd Tom was gonna lose out fer sheriff, sure, Art, but I never knew the story was out that somebody tipped you fellers off to the gold shipments. Jack, where'd you git that story?"

"In Carson. Sheriff there's workin' on it. The murders was done in his territory. Dyer, yuh oughta know somethin' 'bout that."

"Yeah, the story Cameron spread ain't helped. An' I got a hunch him an' Jack're thicker'n fleas on an Injun pup. I'm willin' t' bet money Jack's cashed in on the gold, leavin' the rest o' the gang out in the cold.''

Welch looked at Jack. "You got the ore, Jack— now pay up."

Jack laughed. "When yuh git the split figgered out, I'll bring in the ore and we'll have ol' cheese-cutter Jervis measure it out so we kin each take our cut." He moved the coffee pot back on the fire and filled a dishpan with water.

Art spoke up. "You mean that, Jack?"

"Damn right. Ed figgered on a six-way split. Him an' me an' Art, Welch an' Thompson—Risk was jist a hired gun—Jervis an' Dyer one share. Kit took the gold to Carson an' there it sets. Then we got tipped to another hold-up at the pass. Ed got killed along with Risk an' Thompson, so Art an' me git his share an' that gives us one-half that shipment. Right?"

The men nodded.

"Thompson's share was divided three ways— one fer me, one fer Art, one fer Kit. I agreed t' cash in all the ore fer one third of what Art an' Kit had an' they agreed t' pay off Jervis an' Dyer. Okay, set there an' wrangle! When yuh git it straight, I'll bring in the sacks an' yuh kin split 'em up. I'm sick o' the whole thing!"

The men watched each other. Kit Welch reckoned he might get Jervis and Dyer to sign off, then collect money due him in Carson City. Ben Jervis knew he would be lucky to come out with anything. Art Logan was the only one who sat relaxed.

"Well, boys," Jervis said bravely, "best way is t' take six matches an' make that first box."

The sheriff spoke up. "That's a hell of a penny ante way t' make a split! There's five of us here, let's split it five ways, like it should be."

The silence in the room was broken only by crackling flames, hissing of hot water. Kit Welch spoke, his look as deadly as that of a cat about to jump on a grass clump where a mouse lay hiding. "I'll make it simpler than that, Dyer. Put those matches in three piles. By God, the three of us is all that's left of the bunch that done the work. If Jack an' Art wanta give you fellers somethin' that's up to them."

"Well, there was fifty pounds in the box. Gold's worth twelve dollars an ounce in my store," said Jervis.

Jack cut in. "Jervis, I know somethin' 'bout gold I didn't when our deal was made. Yer figgerin' ten times too high. I found that out in Carson."

Art Logan asked, "Yuh serious, Jack? That bad?"

"Yeah. If yuh want my share, I'll sell it to whoever wants it, cheap!"

Jack moved the dishpan to the back of the stove, slipped in forks, knives and plates. With soft soap on his cloth he swished around in the water, took out the plates and dumped them into a bread pan for rinsing.

Dyer was jawing. "I come up here t' find out a few things. Look t' me like Jack's the only one here tryin' t' act like a white man. That ain't sayin' I b'lieve him, but by grannies he's tryin' t' be fair."

Welch spoke. "Yuh mean I ain't bein' fair?"

"I sure as hell do. If yuh cain't set an' lissen a little, yuh better pull yer freight."

"Yuh think yuh can take me?"

"I know I kin, Welch. Git smart an' I'll blast yuh." The sheriff was on the edge of his chair, hands on knees.

Jack reached for a plate, keeping his eyes on Kit, and put his fingers on a hot pan instead. The pain caused him to knock it to the floor with a bang. Suddenly Welch and Dyer were shooting. The sheriff was hit in the chest, but Welch took a bullet through the ribs and Dyer's second shot centered him. Jervis pulled his derringer and shot at Art Logan, whose answering fire brought Jervis down. He and Art pulled on Dyer, who was still shooting, and both men were dead after that exchange. Jack threw himself on the floor in the corner and waited.

Jervis groaned, belched blood, and slid to the floor. Kit kicked one foot against the table leg time after time. When Jack got up, he saw the hole in his brother's forehead. In the light of the cabin lamp, the survivor looked at death, then walked out into darkness, the last of the Logans, the last of the outlaw gang.

Levi Esch was awakened shortly before midnight by a repeated knock on his door. "I's Jack Logan. I gotta see yuh, Levi."

Levi let him in. Jack walked to a chair and sat down, then looked up at the innkeeper. "Levi, I jist come from the mine. There's been a shootin' up there. The last o' the Logans is settin' right here—the rest of the gang's dead."

"You kill 'em?"

"Nope. About dark Ben Jervis an' Tom Dyer come t' the cabin. They started t' wrangle over their cut in the robberies. Before they was well inta it, Kit an' Art showed up. I seen Kit was on the prod. He got Dyer worked up. I tried t' settle 'em down, but then I dropped a hot pan on the floor accident'ly and it was like sayin' siccem to a buncha dogs. Welch shot Dyer, Dyer shot Welch. Jervis shot Art, Art shot Jervis. Then I reckon Art an' Dyer shot each other. I got down on the floor."

"You never fired?"

"Nope, here's my gun—look an' smell. I brung their ponies—they're in the corral. Yer the closest law. Dyer's dead."

Levi looked at the exhausted outlaw for a long moment. "I'll send fer Cameron and we'll go on up to the mine together," he said.

Esch sent Harry Green pounding out to the Lazy L for Cameron. In Willow Springs, while Cameron ate breakfast, Jack told him what had taken place at the Ajax. There was no living man now to dispute Jack's word.

They rode into Hooper's Bend at dawn, amazed to find the Bar Nothing and Jervis's Mercantile burned to the ground. Hearing what had happened, they were dumbfounded. "Two Mexican men from Mister Logan's mine came into town day before yesterday," MacClure told them. "They showed some gold to one of the girls in the brothel, and came back last night. Flora Miller saw they had plenty to drink, and a wild orgy took place, with everyone drunk—men, women, and girls. In the fancy room with the two Chinese prostitutes, the younger Mexican found he'd been robbed of a piece of gold. He accused a Chinese girl. She couldn't understand what he said. When he got his knife and ran for her, she screamed and jumped out the window to her death. Flora Miller saw him and shot at him. The Mexican went berserk. He stabbed her, cut up the other Chinese girl, and shot out the light. When Mexia ran screaming for help, he broke lamps and started fires in all the drapes.

"I guess he knew he was doomed, and wanted to destroy as much as he could. By the time the men down below got up the stairs it was too late to save anything except the other women and girls. I came when I heard the fire bell. The whole saloon and Flora's place of business was in roaring flames. We tried to save the Mercantile but the wind was against us. Mister Jervis was gone, and so was the sheriff."

Levi Esch spoke up. "They won't come back alive, Mister MacClure. They were shot to death last night up at the Ajax Mine. We come over to pick up someone to go up there with us as witnesses. Welch and Art Logan're dead, too."

MacClure was speechless. The Lord had certainly moved in a mysterious way to clean up Hooper's Bend. "So that's where they were," he said finally.

"Art Logan and Kit Welch done the job, so Jack says. We figgered you an' Cameron would be fair witnesses. We should have one or two more along."

"How about Jerry Dean and Mister Warren?"

"Couldn't find anybody better, Mac," Cameron agreed.

At the cabin, bluejays squalled and fought over scraps thrown out from previous meals. Tracks in the sparse snow showed where horses had stood tied. The cabin door was closed. Jack stayed at the rear of the group. Cameron opened the door and stepped inside, the rest following. In the small room they stood close together to keep from touching the corpses on the floor. Jack stood by the stove.

"Fellers, this is what's left of the bunch held up the stage an' the Blecker kids' wagon. Jervis tipped off Dyer that gold was movin', Dyer tipped off Ed, my brother. We never settled our split. Last night Jervis an' Dyer came up here t' jump me fer money. Then Kit an' Art showed up, unexpected like. Kit was mean, and they was all edgy. I made coffee, fried a few steaks. We argyed about the split all through supper. I thought we could settle it peaceable and was standin' here doin' dishes when a hot pan burnt my fingers an' I dropped it with a bang. All hell broke loose. Kit pulled his gun. Dyer got him, an' he got Dyer. Jervis shot Art and I seen Art open up."

Levi and MacClure checked the guns. Nine shots. Kit Welch had a bullet through his heart. Dyer got a center shot just below his breastbone and another broke his spine. Jervis had been hit once two inches below the collarbone. Art Logan had two bullets in the chest from Jervis's derringer;

Dyer's gun had exploded in his face.

"Jack, it looks like you were right. How do you stand on the robberies?" Cameron asked.

"No part in 'em a-tall. Never knew 'bout the first one till I come in from the Raggeds a couple days later."

"Then why the fuss with Jervis an' Dyer?"

"They thought I handled the ore, but it was Welch took it to Carson. I'll swear for Denny that it's his'n an' he kin claim it."

"What about the High Pass hit and the Blecker boys' murder? Where was yuh then?"

"I was over clost t' the South Fork with a rope and hot iron, come in the day after Art an' Ed got back. I took keer o' Ed till he died. When I got a chance t' deal off the ranch, I took it—I'm shut of the whole caboodle now."

They wrapped the dead men in soogans and horse blankets, laid the bodies over a couple of ponies, and tied them down. Jack took a few things from the cabin, pulled the door shut, then swung on his horse and left.

At Hooper's Bend, the whole town waited. Mrs. Dyer fainted. The shock of the fire and losing the store had already made Mrs. Jervis hysterical. Flora Miller, one Chinese girl, and two men hurt in the fire were being cared for. The Mexican who had stabbed Flora was dead, the other in jail. Men who talked of hanging him before Levi and the rest came back with the dead sheriff and storekeeper now changed their plans and talked of lynching Jack Logan.

Jerry Dean took over. "Fellers, I was up there. I reckon Jack's innocent, so do the rest. I'll take over now until another sheriff's elected. If yuh figger on startin' trouble, yuh got me an' quite a few others t' mix with.''

Douglas MacClure held a town meeting that night, and the ladies from San Francisco were there. They interviewed Nun Chang, the wounded Chinese girl, who told them about the transaction that brought her to Flora's place. Armed with this knowledge, it was easy to get Mexia to admit Flora had put her up to stealing the gold from the Mexicans. Now MacClure had enough information. He would form a committee to rid the town of the madam and her girls.

Hooper's Bend settled down. Talk of the Logans grew less. Two other women came to town to open a brothel. Jerry Dean discouraged them, but he knew that if they didn't stay, someone else would come. It was hard to keep prostitutes out of a cow town.

Percy Cameron and Millie Blecker were married the second week in November. People there thought they had never seen such a pretty bride.

Two weeks later, Jack Logan rode into the ranch, and Denny took him into the kitchen to eat while Mrs. Waldecker went for Cameron. When Percy arrived, Jack sat drinking coffee, eating a piece of pie. ''Fellers, I come t' tell yuh I'm goin' on a short trip down south,'' he said.

''What're your plans, Jack? Gonna bring back a girl?''

''Naw, just wanta wander around a little. Say, how much did that ore Kit took in amount to, anyway?''

"Little over seven hundred and fifty dollars in gold."

"Jervis figgered it'd be four er five thousand. Say, did yuh know he was the one backin' Flory? Yeah, the old shite-poke! He set her up in business and he was the monkey behind a lot o' crooked deals. Hell," Jack went on, "if anything ever happens t' me, that mine goes t' the church. Levi has the paper." He rose, ready to leave. "I reckon if there's a few more summers like this one, we'll be short o' people hereabouts. Four up t' the mine an' two at the Bar Nothin' makes six. Three Bleckers makes nine an' the three at the pass that got killed with 'em makes twelve—all killed this summer. MacClure kin preach quite a sermon on that. Well, thanks fer the grub. Come up t' the Ajax an' see me when yuh kin."

When Jack Logan was heard of again, the news concerned his death. He had been murdered, for gold he carried, in a dive in a southern town called Los Angeles. The murderer implicated a woman, Flora Miller, keeper of a cathouse there. Levi Esch took Jack's will to Douglas MacClure, but only about a hundred pounds of high-grade ore was found at the Ajax.

"Boys," Mr. Denny declared, "I reckon we should take the rest of the powder, set it in front of the tunnel, touch her off, plug it, an' then burn the cabin."

In the years to follow, Douglas MacClure occasionally preached a sermon called "Six Who Died Young." The six were all less than twenty years of age, he said, innocent people destroyed by power and the greed for gold. Five boys and one girl murdered: Loper, Max, and Kiah Blecker; Ming, the Chinese girl; Pedro, the young Mexican; and Jack Logan, ambushed at last by hired outlaws. Death was comonplace where little law existed.

Gold and silver mining continued in Virginia City, the Modoc Uprising occurred in the lava beds, and in the midwest Sioux Indians were on the warpath. As time went by, only the family close to the Blecker boys grieved for and remembered the ones they had lost, and it took thirty years of effort to stamp out the Chinese slave trade in The City by the Golden Gate.

GILES A. LUTZ

Ray Hogan

30801	**Guns Along the Jicarilla**	75¢
47090	**Last Gun at Cabresto**	95¢
51642	**Man From Barranca Negra**	95¢
51643	**Killer's Gun**	95¢
52030	**A Marshal For Lawless**	95¢
84560	**Outside Gun**	$1.25
00000	**Panhandle Pistolero**	$1.25
72370	**The Ridge Runner**	95¢
73600	**Roxie Raker**	95¢
76176	**Showdown On Texas Flat**	95¢
82110	**Trial of the Fresno Kid**	$1.25

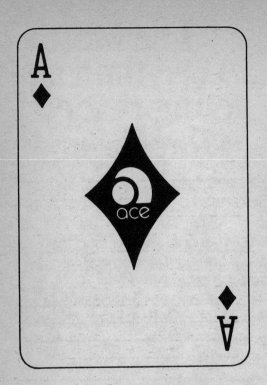